Dear Drama 2

MAR 2014
CH

Dear Drama 2

Dear Drama 2

Braya Spice

www.urbanbooks.net

Urban Books, LLC
97 N18th Street
Wyandanch, NY 11798

ISBN 13: 978-1-60162-404-8
ISBN 10: 1-60162-404-2

First Trade Paperback Printing March 2014
Printed in the United States of America

10 9 8 7 6 5 4 3 2 1

Distributed by Kensington Publishing Corp.
Submit Wholesale Orders to:
Kensington Publishing Corp.
C/O Penguin Group (USA) Inc.
Attention: Order Processing
405 Murray Hill Parkway
East Rutherford, NJ 07073-2316
Phone: 1-800-526-0275
Fax: 1-800-227-9604

Acknowledgments

Hey, all! Thanks for checking back with me again for my second installment of *Dear Drama*. Like Erykah Badu said, "I'm a writer. I'm serious about my shit." LOL. One thing I have always felt is that there is nothing better than being in love . . . Sylvia Plath said, "Love set you going like a fat gold watch." It gives you something to look forward to, make your steps lighter and the things in the world that seem unbearable become more tolerable. The power of love is a prevailing theme in *Dear Drama 2*. One thing I learned when writing this novel is that real love surpasses pain and time. One of the hardest things is trying to still have hope when you have been burnt so many times. The thing I love most about Allure is the fact that she never stopped believing in love despite all she has endured in her quest for it.I'm so excited to bring the characters back from *Dear Drama,* especially James. I'm sure readers hate him with a passion. But there was always just something so dynamic about his relationship with Allure. Without a doubt, he loves Allure. But it is always astounding to me to see people in the world who love someone yet put him or her through so much pain and anguish. I can attest to dealing with this. And in writing the closing chapter, I broke down bawling, because in all actuality I struggled with how to properly end this story. I don't want to give it away, but boy, oh, boy, does Allure have a dilemma! And you know Allure wouldn't be Allure if there wasn't a fair share of drama. So sit back and enjoy

Acknowledgments

it. I wrote it from the heart. Single mothers, I wrote this for you. Pease don't give up hope. Be the best you can be and continue to believe that you deserve wholesome, mind blowing mind. Aim for it, accept no less than this! You deserve this!

I want to thank my children, Adara and Bralynn. Love you two!

Thanks to my mother and my sister, Crystal. Look out for my sister's hair-care line, called Luxe Therapy! It is doing big things.

Hey to my nieces, Mikayla and Maydison; my nephews, Omari and Jeff Jr.; my cousins Donnie, Devin, and Mu-Mu; and my goddaughter, La'naya. Hey to Tammy, Shauntae, Ray, and Eric.

Thanks to my friends Sheryl, Shawnda, Gwen, Christina, Linda, Tracy, Christina T, Talamontes, Pam, Carla, Sewiaa, Ronisha (RIP), Shumeka, Valerie Hoyt, Tara, Pearlean, Maxine, Dena, Barbara, Henrietta, Candis, VI, Phillipo, Latonya, Leigh, Yvonne Gayner, Ivy, and Daphne.

Thanks to Patrice! You adopted me as your baby sister. Thank you so much for always being there for me. No matter the problem or how much pain I feel, your words always have the power to cure me. And here's a shout-out to some supporters, Sandy, Papaya, Bernie, Sharlene Johnna and Charlotte.

I will get a karate chop if I don't say this. I would like to dedicate *Dear Drama 2* to Mr. Apacacio, aka Detective Mateo.

Thanks to Carl and Natalie.

Thanks to my editor, Kevin Dwyer. We are on again. Yes!

Special thanks go out to my fans. Muah!

Dear Drama is bizzack! Enjoy.

Finally

He is everything without trying.
Fulfilling every wish without lying.
There's a sting from a constant pinch-Cause
I'm telling myself . . . This has to be a dream.
He came nowhere but that nowhere has surely blessed
me with a man I've waited my whole life
He's the epitome of what every man should be.
There's a beauty about this man that
can never be replicated
Butterflies are immediately apparent,
in in the pit of my tummy when he is near.
Lord what can I say? He loves me without
hesitation or limitation.
Does not try to change me but accepts me as I am.
On hellish days that seem to deliberately
pull me to pieces, you pick them on up
and recoup me. I know few women have this and
when it's time to break it down,
I have a lack of terminology
to disclose A man of your caliber.
That is because all words are understatements.
To your tremendous attributes.
My soul's at ease-days can fly by, I'm content.
A rainy day is sheer enjoyment. Rush hour
traffic don't bother me much.
And I feel so at home.
Strangers, they tell me my smile's lovely.
Happiness apparent. Seeing the sun
before I even open my eyes.
Cause this man, he's true and he's loving me . . .
Finally . . . .

Prologue

I was so excited to go on this road trip with Derek! *It's a good thing that things didn't work out between him and his girlfriend,* I thought. We were taking a trip to a resort in Palm Springs.

During most of the drive, he was pretty quiet. But he kept passing smiles my way and grabbing my hand and squeezing it.

Then, out of nowhere, as we were enjoying the new Eric Roberson CD, he asked me, "Soooo, Allure, no baby's daddy drama?"

I offered a smile at that comment. But I didn't want to speak on negative things. He started talking before I could, anyway.

"Lords knows I have my share of drama. My baby's mama is a real trip. You know, I gave her what her heart desired, and she gave me a hard time. She complains about this, she complains about that, but all she does is sit on her fat punk ass and eat Krispy Kreme Doughnuts. Fucking bitch."

That is harsh, I thought. It was a side of Derek that I had never seen. But wait. . . . There was more. . . .

"Are you still sleeping with your baby's father?"

"Excuse me?"

He bit on his lip, as if he wanted to punish himself for letting that question slip out. "It's just that I noticed people who have a child with someone don't really have enough willpower to just let the relationship go completely."

I looked out the window and shifted my body closer to the passenger door. I didn't like where the conversation was going.

"I'm sure you know what I'm talking about, Allure." He passed me a look, then turned his attention to the interstate we were on.

"No, I really can't say that I do."

"Oh, when that nigga comes over with a bag of damn diapers for a child he ain't seen in four months and your real man is out working, one thing leads to another. Those old feelings come back. You giving him becky!"

"Look, I'm not comfortable with this conversation." And now I was second-guessing if I should have come with him.

He looked at me, surprised. "I asked you a simple fucking question, and you want to bite my goddamned head off. Get the fuck out!"

"What?"

"I said get the fuck out. You crazy bitch."

He pulled over quickly, almost causing the truck to tip over, grabbed my purse, and threw it my way. It dropped to the floor, and all my stuff fell out of it. I had no choice but to scoop it back inside and follow the finger that pointed to my exit. Without saying anything, I unfastened my seat belt, stood up from the seat, opened the door, and stepped out of the truck. He slammed the door behind me.

Now, first off, I didn't know where I was, and I had no way to get my ass home. Almost immediately, I was hit with a gust of wind that shot my dress in the air. Nearby truckers howled and whistled their approval. I crossed my arms over my cold body and walked away with tears burning under my eyelids. Once again, I thought, I didn't know how the fuck I was going to get home, if I could make it there at all.

There wasn't much around me, but about twenty feet away were some benches and pay phones. Who could I call this time of night? Better yet, who could come all this way to pick me up?

I screamed when I saw a body huddled on a bench. When he looked my way, he smiled, soothing me. He looked no older than me, and he was wrapped in a raggedy yellow blanket.

"Hello," he said.

"Hi. Do you know where we are?"

"The desert," was all he said.

I grabbed my cell out of my purse to call my mother, but as her phone rang, I changed my mind. This would give her a heart attack. I couldn't call her. I called my sister instead.

She was groggy when she answered, and most likely, annoyed someone was calling her so late.

"Crystal, it's kind of an emergency. I need you to come pick me up."

"She's not gonna find you out here," the guy warned.

"Who is that?" Crystal asked.

"No one. Look, like I said, I'm kinda stranded, okay?"

"Okay. Where are you?"

"Some—"

Someone tapped me on the back.

It was Derek. I held the phone like a weapon, ready to crack his ass with it.

"Get the fuck away from me!" I yelled.

I heard my sister scream my name on the phone.

"I'm sorry," Derek said.

"You're sick," I muttered.

"No. I'm sorry. Give me the phone."

"No."

He snatched it out of my hand. "Hello? How are you? Oh, you're her sister? Nice to meet you. I'm a friend of

Allure's. Listen, everything is fine. We just got into a little argument. We both said some things that were wrong, but I'm back. I'm going to feed Allure and get her home safely. Trust me, everything is going to be okay. Get some rest."

He turned back to me and said, "Allure, I'm very sorry. I didn't mean that stuff. I want you to come with me, okay? Now, tell your sister everything is fine."

Truth was, where we were, how easy would it be for her to find me? We were in the middle of nowhere. So I accepted that I would need to ride home with this dick.

I gave him a mean look and took the phone. "Crystal."

"Allure, what the fuck is going on?"

"Never mind, Crystal."

"Listen to me. If you're not home by seven a.m., I'm calling the fucking police. Do you hear me? Do you?" she shouted.

My whole body was shivering. "Yes, Crystal." I put the receiver back on the post.

"Like I said, I'm sorry. Come on. Let's go."

I didn't want to leave with Derek, but what the guy on the bench had said had me a little afraid. What if I couldn't be found out here? Hesitantly, I followed behind him.

"I'm sorry I couldn't help you," the guy offered.

I turned to face him. "I'm sorry I couldn't help you."

"Bye," he said, smiling.

I smiled back at him and turned back around to follow Derek. When we made it back to the truck, he stopped and faced me. "You know, I can't believe you."

"What?"

"You can talk to a fucking homeless man, but your ass can't talk to me? He could be damn crazy. You smiling at his ass and shooting venom my fucking way like a snake!" He shook his head suddenly. "No! What am I doing?" He grabbed both my arms. "I'm sorry, Allure. Look at me, baby."

I did, and I found myself looking into the eyes of a madman, a black Jack the Ripper. *I may not make it past the night,* I thought. And it would serve me right for doing something so damn dumb!

"Do you trust me?"

I fibbed with a nod, although I could think of places I would have felt safer. Like a KKK convention or a lion's den.

"Listen, I don't want you to get back into the truck until you feel safe and know I'm not going to hurt you, okay?"

I nodded again, although I didn't feel safe with him.

"Okay, baby, come on in."

I obeyed, and once seated, I buckled my seat belt. He did the same.

Once on the road, he asked me, "Is there any way I can make this up to you?"

I refrained from comment.

The ride there wasn't much farther, according to him. I politely asked his permission to go and lie down in the back.

"Go ahead. We'll get food in about thirty minutes."

His cell phone rang. "Whasssup? Yes, I'm coming to his party. I gave you three hundred already. I'm not giving you any more money for a goddamned cotton candy machine. Whatever. Bye." He slammed the phone down.

"That's my baby's mom, always trying to milk my ass for money. I hope you ain't like that."

I refrained from comment again.

"She is always bitching and demanding shit from me. As if I don't do enough for my son as it is. I don't know how I ended up with her big ass. All she was ever concerned with was what I could give her ass. I paid all her bills, sent flowers to her job every damn week, and you know what she did to me?"

His eyes were shooting fire. I almost jumped. "No, I don't."

"She used one of my credit cards, bought a new car, and ran off with another nigga!"

"I'm sorry to hear that."

"No, you ain't."

Okay. Then, shit, I wasn't.

"You know what I realized? I need me a damn woman. I'm tired of being alone. I don't have anyone to come home to. All I want is to come home to my woman and cook a couple of Cornish hens, some potatoes, and corn muffins."

The thought of food made my stomach lurch.

"Then, after we chow down, we go on in the room and I eat that pussy till it's so clean, you could put in back on the shelf!"

I once again refrained from comment.

"I'm tired of being alone. I sit there and buy them dumb magazines and spend all my time jacking off! Shit, for the price of an *Ebony Humpers,* I could get my girl's nails done! Tell me something, Allure. What's wrong with me?"

"You a fucking nut job," I wanted to say, but instead, I shrugged. "I don't know."

"Yeah. You ain't shit special," he quipped.

I sighed.

"Do you think I'll get another chance to see you again, Allure?"

"I really don—"

"I can imagine what you're going to tell your family when you get back. You'll probably tell them that I raped you and everything else." My eyes got wide when he held up a condom and a gun. "Because that is what I intend to do! Go back there and get naked!"

I screamed at the top of my lungs.

Ring! Ring!

My eyes shot open, and my heart was pounding out of my chest. I snatched up my cell phone and blindly answered it. "Hello?"

Thank God that shit was a nightmare! If I would sit in the truck of a man who said all that crazy shit and would not at any moment try to get away—even if I had to open the door, jump, and do a tuck and roll—hell, I needed to be sliced and diced. I thanked God the new me wouldn't do any crazy spontaneous stuff like that for love.

I glanced at the caller ID on my phone. It was my mother. She never called me this late.

"Hello?"

"Allure, listen. Something very bad happened. I need you to meet me over at Bellflower Medical Center as soon as you can."

I immediately panicked. Sierra and my sister had gone to the movies to see *Breaking Dawn—Part 2*. I had been planning on going too, but I had a bad cold and had ended up taking some medicine that knocked me out. "What? To who, Mom?"

"There was a bad car accident. Just get over here."

My hands would not stop shaking as I raced over to the hospital. My mother's words played over and over in my head. I wiped away tears nervously as I drove, not knowing what to expect. No. I knew what to expect . . . that this could be a very, very bad situation. My baby and my sister could be really hurt or worse.

I parked on the street outside of Bellflower Medical Center.

My heart thumped wildly in my chest as I jumped out of my car and raced to the emergency room double doors. I tried to stay calm. I saw my mother standing not far from me, talking to a doctor. I wasn't close enough to hear what he said, but whatever it was caused my mother to collapse. I took off running, sobbing and yelling, "Mama! What is it?"

By the time I made it to her, she was screaming at the top of her lungs, "No! Not my baby!"

"Mama! Doctor! What happened? I'm Sierra's mom and Crystal's sister. Please tell me!"

"Sierra is fine." He took a deep breath. "But . . ."

"But what?" I demanded. But as my mother continued to shout, "Not my baby," I knew what his next words were going to be even before he said them. And it crushed me.

"Your sister died. I'm sorry."

"My sister . . . my sister is dead?" I whispered.

The doctor nodded. "I'm afraid so."

I covered my face with my hands and bawled like a baby into them. I felt like the walls were closing in on me. I ended up on the floor, next to my mother, and went from bawling to screaming.

Chapter 1

Although Sierra was now nine years old, I didn't want her at my sister's funeral. My sister had always been like a best friend to me. I couldn't imagine life without her. The days leading up to the funeral, I was sent back to the hospital and sedated so much, it was crazy. Coping with her death was not an easy feat. I knew people said that time healed all wounds, but for me a chunk of my heart was missing because I had lost her. The love of my daughter was what kept me going. I had always had to be strong for her. I knew this. But that shit was hard. Life was hard as hell, especially when you were trying to live it without the people you never thought you'd have to live it without.

I knew today would be so hard for me. She would finally be laid to rest.

During the service, my mother was completely out of it. I knew the doctor had given her something before the service, or else she wouldn't be able to get through it. But still she struggled.

I struggled through the service as well. As several people talked, I cried silently and thought of happier times with my sister. I thought of how she was always there for me when I needed her and never offered me any type of judgment. How she was such a good aunt to little Sierra from day one. And all that did was make me feel worse. My sister would have no kids of her own. When it was time to go up to the casket, I freaked out, and instead

I ran out of the funeral home, sobbing all the way to the limo. I sat in it by myself and continued to cry.

Once the service was over, I managed to make it over to the grave site, despite the fact that I wanted to go the other way. I knew this was a day I had to get through, although I didn't want to. My mother didn't make it, though. After I ran out of the church, my mother passed out. Poor mama. As they lowered my sister into the ground, and I watched from the chair I was seated in, I asked myself again, *Why do I have to keep going through pain? First, I lose my dad, my son, and now I lose my sister.* My lips trembled as they covered her casket with dirt. Tears continued to pour from my eyes.

Soon people began to leave. I glanced at the spot where my sister was now buried. I sobbed and covered my face with my hands.

Why do I have to keep going through shit? I demanded silently.

Suddenly, someone removed my hands from my face. My eyes shot open, and I spied James!

He knelt down in front of me. "Hey, Allure." He used some tissue to wipe the tears and snot off of my face.

Too emotional, I didn't stop him. In fact, I was so emotional that I threw myself in his arms and let him hold me.

"How are you holding up, baby?" He stroked my back.

It did feel good to have someone hold me. I hadn't been held in so long. But still, after a few seconds I demanded calmly, "What are you doing here?"

"I heard your sister had passed. I couldn't let you deal with this on your own. I had to come and be there for you, baby."

I narrowed my eyes at him. Our family and friends didn't travel in the same circles. So how could he have known about my sister? I wondered.

"How did you know?" I asked him.

"I just did, baby."

"How? And stop calling me baby please."

"Your Facebook."

My Facebook page was private. Only my friends could see my personal business. Yes, I had put info about my sister's funeral on my page, but James wasn't a friend of mine on Facebook. Or was he?

"To keep it all the way real, ba . . . Allure, I have a different name on there. I requested you a few years back. I just wanted to have a way to keep in contact with you. See how you were doing. And you seem to be doing well. I see you finished school. You are a teacher, which judging by your pictures, you seem to love. You bought your own home. . . . And Sierra. Man, she is a big girl now, and so pretty. I'm proud as hell of you, baby." He paused before saying, "You're not mad I did that, are you?"

Does this man ever change? James was my ex, and boy, was it a bad breakup. Talk about breaking my heart. He smashed it, then lit it on fire. It had been three years since I had seen him last. I could never forget how he slept with me and then went and married the same girl who he had cheated on me with while I was carrying his child. Nor could I forget how he had left me after our son died. The list of how foul he had been to Sierra and me went on and on.

"I am. But right now I don't have the time to be concerned about you're stalking, because that's what it is, James." I glanced over at my sister's grave site again. I moaned and felt more tears slide down my face.

"Baby, I know this is hard for you. You loved your sister. I just came to make sure you—"

My older brother, Bobby, walked up. He had brown skin and was tall and lanky like my father. We actually looked a lot alike. He gave James a friendly nod before saying, "Allure, the limo is about to leave. You need to come on so we can go back to Mama's house."

I stood to my feet and took steps toward my brother. I didn't turn and look at James. He was the least of my concerns right now. I needed to focus on getting through this day.

I heard James calling my name, but I ignored him and kept walking.

"Who is that?" my brother asked.

"No one important."

During the wake, I sat in a corner and watched as food was passed around. I had no appetite for any of it. Although the wake was held at my mother's house, she wasn't there. Both my brothers were and a few family members who lived in California. A lot of my sister's friends were present, and her clients from her hair salon as well. Everyone looked somber. When people came up to me and offered me a hug, I took it, but when they tried to talk to me, I politely told them I wasn't feeling well and wanted to lie down. I went to my mother's room and lay on her bed. Sad thoughts filled me yet again. I couldn't believe that my sister was gone. That was the crazy part about life. Each day there was no guarantee you'd live another day. But once you died, you were guaranteed not to walk the earth again. Life wasn't permanent. Death was.

Thing was, I could sit in denial, because the situation was crazy as hell and so cliché that it couldn't possibly be true. Could a young, drunk-ass driver really have crashed into my sister's truck and instantly killed her? Come the fuck on. The drunk driver was in a car, and my sister was in a truck? And the drunk-ass driver suffered only a broken arm, while my sister was the casualty? I could entertain denial just based on how crazy the shit sounded. As crazy as it was . . . it was reality. My big sis was gone. All the crying and the sad thoughts I had had my head pounding and my throat dry.

I got up and left the room to get some water. When I stepped into the living room, I saw my mother had come back. She was in the kitchen, sobbing. I saw one of my brother hugging her. I couldn't take any more crying if I was going to control my own tears, so I snuck out of the living room, grabbed my purse and keys, and left my mother's house.

Chapter 2

I drove past my mother's house and headed toward Long Beach Boulevard, heading to Tobo's, a local hole-in-the-wall bar. I parked quickly, jumped out of my car, walked inside, and slipped onto a bar stool. As soon as the bartender came up to me, I said, "Send me four vodkas and cranberry juices." I slid him my credit card so he could start a tab for me. He gave me an odd look while doing so.

A few minutes later, he slid all four glasses in front of me. I picked up one glass and downed it, ignoring the burning of the alcohol as it slipped down my throat. I went to the next glass and did the same. Then I went to the third drink. I swallowed that one down as well. I started feeling loose and tingly. My racing thoughts were dissipating. I was feeling warm and fuzzy.

"Allure."

I turned around slowly and saw James. What the fuck did he want now? I stared him down as he sat on the stool next to me.

"Why are you here again? I left you at the funeral home for a reason. I want you to leave me the fuck alone."

"What are you doing here, baby?"

"What does it look like I'm doing here, James?"

"You're drinking, baby. But—"

"Exactly. I'm drinking. I'm getting fucked up. I'm trying to feel numb. Not feel a damn thing. And I'm almost there, and then here you come. Fuck!"

"Well, I followed you over to the wake. I started to come in but didn't know if it would be okay, since you left me at the cemetery. So I waited outside, just to make sure that you were okay. Then I saw you drive away, so I followed you."

I hadn't been at my mother's house that long. But still . . . James was acting weird as hell.

What a stalker, I thought. As he continued to talk, saying how nice I looked, I blocked out his words and downed half of my fourth drink. I was getting seriously fucked up.

"Besides all the things you have accomplished, Allure, how are you doing in the love department?" I heard him say.

I pierced him with a glare. I could not believe he was asking me about my personal life after all the foul stuff he had done to me.

"My bad, baby. Maybe I'm taking this a bit too far. Let me show you something." He pulled out his iPhone, put in a code, and started showing me pictures of two adorable little boys. Boys that looked just like him. "Ryder is three, and JJ is a year old."

I looked away and nodded. "Congratulations." I wondered if he ever thought about Jeremiah.

Suddenly, I felt one of his hands on my face and his other hand over my hand that was holding my fourth drink.

"Let me help you. You don't need to be in this bar alone. There are too many crazy and dirty muthafuckas here that could hurt you. You are not in your right mind right now. You are vulnerable, hurt. Look, you don't need to be around nobody but me. Let me take you home, make you some tea, and put you to bed, baby. I'm not trying to get anything from you. Despite all the fucked-up stuff that happened between you and me, I still care about you." His eyes locked with mine. "Deeply. I just want to make sure you are okay. Then, once I get you in bed, safe, baby, I'll bounce." He gestured toward all the glasses. "You are in no condition to drive. And Sierra needs you. And I know this has to be hard. I can't imagine how I would feel if I lost my brother."

The good feelings the liquor had imparted stopped when I was once again reminded of what had gone on earlier that day. . . . I had buried my big sister. I took one look at him, and I broke down crying again, not caring at the moment if he saw me as weak and not caring that I had a lot of hatred for him. I was hurting too badly.

"Awww, baby. Let it out. That's the only way you are going to heal from this." He started hugging me and ran his hands up and down my back. I was hurting so bad that I welcomed his embrace.

When he helped me to my feet, I didn't protest, as much as I detested him. But he was right. I was in no condition to drive home.

Once we arrived at my house, James helped me inside. He was right about one thing. I had had entirely too much to drink. He helped me out of my shoes, stockings, and my dress. He found my nightgown and helped me into it. He brought me a mug of tea.

"Sit up, baby."

I did, and he handed me the mug of tea. I blew on the top of the mug, waited a few seconds, and then I sipped the tea.

"You feeling a little better, babe?"

I wasn't, but I nodded. I placed the mug on the nightstand near me.

He pulled out his cell phone, glanced at it, and said, "Well, let me get going."

A feeling of alarm hit me. I didn't want to spend this night alone. I figured I was entitled to using whatever diversions I could get my hands on just to get through the night.

He leaned over and kissed me on my cheek. As he pulled away, he said, "If you or Sierra needs anything, give me a—"

I grabbed his hand and caused him to halt his speech. I broke down crying again. "I know I shouldn't be saying this. You're a married man with two kids, but . . ."

"Just say it, baby," he urged gently.

"Please stay with me tonight, James. Please."

He did not hesitate. He yanked off his shoes and crawled into the bed. "Of course I will, Allure." He spooned me from behind. He wrapped his arms around me and kissed me on my neck. Then he started humming Beyoncé's song *I Miss You.*

I knew the song very well, and whenever I heard it, it brought me back to him. And every time the song ended, I was in tears, wishing that things had ended differently between us. Wishing that he would magically appear on my doorstep without a wedding band on. That day had never come. And I remembered always feeling so horrible that I wouldn't want to get out of bed. I had no energy and often just wanted to collapse. What he had done had put me into a deep depression, one that I had to fight my way out of.

Yet, after all of this, it was funny that, even though I hadn't lain with this man in three years, I felt as though no real time had passed between us. Most of the pain had left. Not all of it, but most of it. But the love was still there. I felt like I was back at my old apartment and he was holding me and he was mine.

But we weren't there anymore. Yet my heart still was. Which was exactly why when he said his next words, I should have said no. But I didn't.

He kissed me on my cheek, and his lips and teeth bumped against my earlobe. "Let me make you feel good, baby. Just for tonight. Then I'll leave in the morning, and we can pretend that this day never existed."

"Yes, please."

That was all it took before his mouth devoured mine. He then pulled me out of my nightgown and kissed me on every single part of my body. From my face to my neck, my shoulders to my waist and then my knees, and then from my knees to my feet. Then he turned me over. He left no spot on my body untouched.

He then spread my legs apart and started eating my pussy. He was just as good as I remembered. He used his tongue and let it flicker over my clit; then he licked up and down my opening, started suckling and driving me insane. He fingered my insides while he went back to licking on my clit. My legs started to shake. He rearranged us so that I was on top of him. He fingered my breasts, and I rode him. I closed my eyes and focused on how good it felt to have him inside my walls again.

After three fucking years.

He used one hand to control my movements, gripping the right side of my waist and yanking me down at a faster rate. His other hand continued to tease my nipples, alternating between both rather quickly.

I moaned and tossed back my head.

He pulled my face down and tried to kiss me. But I wouldn't let him. I turned my face, and he ended up kissing my cheek.

I twisted and ground my body over him until he flipped me over, placed one of my legs over his shoulder, and drilled me while sucking on one of my nipples. I moaned and thrashed my head from side to side. He was hitting my spot and driving me insane.

"Let it out, baby."

I felt my orgasm coming on. It made me clench my teeth and my legs shiver. James started pounding harder and faster, letting me know he was on the brink of coming as well. He gripped my breasts in his hands and let out a loud moan. Then he collapsed on my chest. Neither of us said anything about what we had just done. I didn't even give myself a chance to feel stupid or foul for sleeping with a now married man. I simple rolled over on my side, and James cuddled me close. And as soon as I recovered, I asked him to have sex with me again and again, until I grew weak and fell asleep.

What was it about a man that made a woman feel comforted? For me, no matter what I was dealing with, a man could provide a sort of comfort that no one else could.

Chapter 3

The phone ringing woke me out of my sleep. I ignored it, and after the fourth ring, it stopped. I placed a hand on my head, which was aching. *Shit.* When I felt a movement in my bed, I froze. Then, like a movie, the memories of the night before unfolded in front of me. My body shifted, and the arm wrapped around my waist gripped me tighter. I turned my head slightly and looked at James. He was sleeping so peacefully and had not a care in the world.

I, on the other hand, had plenty. My sister was put to rest yesterday, for starters, and no matter how bad I felt about it and how good it felt to fuck him the night before, the fact of the matter was that he was now a married man and my punk ass was in serious violation. After he dropped me off last night, the truth was, I should have sent him home. I should have never let him step foot in my house. But I was now grown up enough to know that I really shouldn't bother with shoulda, coulda, woulda. And I knew I needed to own when I fucked up. It was a part of growing. And Lord knows, I fucked up. I could see an image of black Jesus shaking his head at me while sitting on a cloud. I tried to pull away from James, and he tightened his arm around me again.

"James."

He kissed me on my cheek and moaned low in his throat.

I nudged him with an elbow. "James!"

"Huh?" He jumped and sat up slightly. "What's wrong, baby?" He rubbed his hands up and down my arms. I scooted over in the bed, away from him, toward the edge.

"You know we fucked up last night, right?"

My phone started ringing again.

Without a second of hesitation, he asked, "Are you going to get your phone?"

"No." Whoever was calling could wait.

"Do you want me to get it for you?"

"No."

"Why don't you want to answer it, Allure? Is it someone that you don't want me to know is calling?"

I gave him a crazy look.

He actually had the nerve to have a jealous expression on his face. "Is it another nigga, baby? Keep it all the way real."

"What? Look, you doing a bit fucking much, James! The fact that you fucked my brains out last night doesn't change the bad blood between you and me. Or give you the right to question what the fuck I do."

He shook his head confidently. "Allure, maybe you hate me, but I, baby, I love—"

I put one of my hands over his mouth before he could finish his sentence. "Would you stop this fucking insanity!" I poked him in his chest with one on my fingers. "You have a wife and two small boys. I had no business doing what I did with you. It's wrong! I'm no better than her when she was fucking with you and I was with you."

"Baby, you were in a vulnerable state last night. That's why you did it. You were drunk and hurt about your sister. That's why I positioned myself the way I did. I couldn't bear the thought of you taking home one of those nothing-ass niggas at the bar. You would have regretted that shit."

"More than I regret this?"

"They could have hurt you. Come on, baby. Forget about that. Let me love you. Lie down and let me love on you some more."

He was not fucking getting it! "James, no! Shut up with that."

"Well, damn, what did you want me to do, baby? I was concerned about you. I got you through the day. I know I shouldn't have slept with you, because I'm in a marriage that I don't want to be in. I mean, I had the opportunity to soothe the woman that I really—"

"Okay, that's it." I stood to my feet and searched for my nightgown. "You need to leave, James. Now!"

He huffed out a deep breath but remained seated on my bed.

"James!" I shoved him until he was on his back.

He stood to his feet, nude, and towered above me. He had a frustrated scowl on his face and backed me into the corner until my back and the backs of my calves were touching the wall.

When he saw my wide eyes, his face softened. "Look, Allure, I know what you thinking about this shit, but that ain't it. . . . And yeah, it's not a good look for me to make love to you—"

"No. We fucked."

"No, we made love. I fuck her. But like I was saying, it was wrong when I have a wife. But forget about what happened three years ago, when I propositioned you at the restaurant. You're back there right now. That's what's in your eyes. But last night, all I had was sincere intentions toward you. I was really worried, and I just wanted to be there for you. Seeing you cry makes me want to cry. I wish I could take your hurt and put it in me. I wish I could do all the grieving. But things aren't that simple. I can't help the fact that I still got you in my heart.

"Sometimes I wish I had got you pregnant the last time we slept together before I got married, so I had a reason to stick around, to call you, to check up on you forever. Baby, I never got over you. But I do take responsibility for making this shit such a big fucking mess with my bad decisions. And I don't care how much time passes, whether it's three, five, ten years. I'm never going to want you to be with anyone else, 'cause I still want you. I know that makes me a selfish-ass man. But at least it's the truth. And when does a woman get that?"

I didn't know if I believed James. Yeah, the shit sounded good. And to know that he still cared for me was cool. But he had lied to me and abused my trust so many times in the past, I would be a fool to just believe him. But I still loved and wanted him. So as his hands rubbed up and down my arms and he kissed my lips, it made me weak again. I tried to pull away, but he was keeping me prisoner in the corner. I should also add that I had been celibate for the past three years.

"James, stop," I said firmly.

He kissed my lips again and whispered, "Okay."

"Please get dressed and go home."

He nodded, looking my nude body up and down with lust and approval in his eyes. James had always had a way of making me feel like I was the prettiest girl in the world.

I continued to search for my nightgown. I saw it underneath my bed. I bent over, grabbed it, and slipped it on. When I turned around, I saw James had my cell phone in his hand.

"What are you doing?"

"Nothing."

He sat it on the nightstand, where it had been. Then he started getting dressed.

Suddenly I heard the doorbell. I walked out of my bedroom, down the hall, and to the front door. When I opened it, I discovered it was Creole.

I knew she wasn't going to come to the funeral. She had said she just didn't "do dead people." But she had sent platters of food to the wake. Kendra, my other close friend who had just had a baby a week before, so she was home with her new baby and her hubby Sierra was in tow. Kendra had been married for the past two years. My girl had hit the jackpot and had found love. I was so happy for her. Sierra was a flower girl and I was the maid of honor at her wedding.

"Bitch! If Mammouth won't come to the motherfucking phone and shit! I had to come see if you had ended your shit!"

Creole had always had a way of making me laugh, despite what I was dealing with. But given the situation, this time, she managed to get only a smile out of me. "Its if Mammouth won't come to the mountain stupid."

"Whatever! I'm saying, bitch, I been blowing up your phone."

"Sorry. I—"

Her eyes suddenly widened. She was looking behind me.

She looked from him to me. Then she gave him a dirty look. Then, as if she was saying, "Slut!" she looked at me.

James flashed her a smile and said, "How you been, Creole?"

"Nigga! We ain't cool."

He shrugged indifferently at that part. James was so arrogant that he never cared if my family or friends didn't like him. It meant nothing to him. He had said that all he ever needed was my and Sierra's approval.

"Matter a fact, why the fuck you here?" Creole muttered.

"Allure needed me to be here—"

Creole shook her head. "James, please! All you ever cared about was yourself."

He ignored her and said to me, "Here is your phone. Give this to baby girl for me." He slid a hundred-dollar bill and my cell into my hand. He then kissed my cheek and walked out the door.

I was left standing in front of Creole, while she contin-ued to look from the door to me.

"Now, I don't want to go crazy on you, seeing that you had to bury your sister yesterday, but what in the fuck was that man doing here?"

I sat down on the couch in my living room. Creole re-mained standing with her arms crossed under her chest.

"I know what you thinking, Creole. I fucked up." I buried my face in the palms of my hands. I had sworn never to have anything else to do with James, and I had slept with him. I was truly dumb.

She sat down next to me. "I'm not going to sit here and judge you, Allure. I know your heart. And I also think that what you going through is hard as fuck, so however you gotta get through it, do it, 'cause no one can feel your pain. That's not my concern. My concern is you going through *more* pain. And that's that motherfucka's middle name—pain!"

I nodded. I couldn't argue with the shit she was saying.

"Where did you see his ass at?"

I went over how he was one of my Facebook friends and I didn't even know the shit.

"That mothafucka."

"He has two beautiful boys." I shook my head, thinking, *Stupid, stupid, stupid, I am.*

"Man, it's done. You have no interest in seeing him again, right? It was just a one-time thing?"

I nodded. But as I did so, flashbacks of the night before percolated in my head, making me question whether I was really done with him. I was, I told myself.

"Okay, then, we off the dick. How are you holding up about your sister?"

I closed my eyes briefly and nodded. "I'm doing a lot better today, now that we laid her to rest. But I tell you, there is nothing more traumatic than watching someone put someone you love in the ground. I had to get fucked up to digest that shit. Seeing her in that casket was hard. To live life like a sane person, you are forced to accept they ain't coming back. And if you refuse to accept it, you crazy. I mean, it makes sense because it's reality that my sister is dead. But the shit is hard and unreasonable as hell. She didn't sign up for that shit."

I felt tears slip from my eyes. I took a deep breath. "But I know Sierra needs me, so I have to pull it together, like I had to pull it together when Jeremiah died. So don't worry about me. I will."

I got a text on my cell phone. It was from James. It read, Baby, this is my number. If you or Sierra needs anything, hit me up.

I rolled my eyes.

"What?"

"Nothing. It's Greg," I lied. Greg was Sierra's father.

"Oh. What I was going to tell you is, you done been through some shit, girl. I don't know if I could have handled all that you have. I probably would have ended it or killed somebody. I probably would have done both. Or some AK-forty-seven-type shit!"

I laughed at her craziness.

She looked relieved that I was even able to laugh.

"You going to be all right, Allure."

"Thanks, Creole."

She leaned over and hugged me. I knew she wasn't an emotional type of female, so I appreciated that she bent her rules for me.

Chapter 4

Getting back into my regular rituals was also a good way to heal. I started back at work. I was working at Gardena High School. I had learned while I was getting my credential that if you agreed to work at an inner-city school, they paid off your school loans. I guess they needed to bribe people. To be honest, I didn't care where I taught. I was just happy that I was given the chance to do what I had always dreamed of doing: teach literature and creative writing classes. I loved it. I also loved how Sierra looked up to me. She bragged to all her friends that her mommy was a teacher and that we owned our own house. It was such a good feeling.

Being a teacher gave me the time to pick my daughter up from school, the energy to make a home-cooked meal, and the opportunity to help Sierra with her homework. I had bought a small house in North Long Beach. It was a two bedroom. Nothing spectacular, but it had a huge backyard, was on a quiet street, and the shit was mine. All my neighbors were cool. In fact, my neighbor who lived two houses down had a son who went to Sierra's school, so if she ever needed to, she could get a ride with them. But I always took my baby girl to school. Sierra was still doing well in school and was playing basketball.

Greg was still around. And I was thankful he was honoring our agreement and was leaving me the hell alone to live my life. I mean, every now and then I would get a phone call from him, and he'd say something stupid like,

"Allure, I miss us" or "Let's get back together, go at this shit called life right." But I never paid him any mind. He would forever be Sierra's father. But he would forever be in my past. I just wished he would be consistently in Sierra's life. He was also forever letting her down. And just to get to the point were at now was not easy in the least. It took an act of Congress aka the courts for me to even let Greg near my child. But after the neglect he subjected her to the judge assisted me with the task of making things safer for my child. I thought back to the another time I wanted to kill Greg because he was so irresponsible with my child. I thought back to right after I graduated from college. My sister and I took a trip to Atlanta: The whole reason I tried my damndest to keep Greg out of our life and let to a battle in court.

It was the first time I had ever been out of state and it was a treat for my graduating college. Initially, I wanted to take my daughter with me but my sister had other plans for us. "Girl are you crazy! We going to the ATL the last thing you want to do in the ATL is bring a kid. We going there to get ratched! We planned to stay for five days. Due to my mother's work schedule she was unable to keep Sierra. So Greg argeed to keep Sierra. I was a little hesitant but Greg swore to me over the phone that Sierra would be fine. But I don't know . . . Ever since the fiasco with Angel I never let Sierra spend more than a day or two at his mother's house. Never five days. "Allure. A lot has changed in my life. I got saved at church and baptized. I'm working now and everything. You are not going to have any more problems out of me. And Sierra will be safe in my care. You know I'm still staying with my mother so she will be there too and you know she is not going to let anything happen to her only grandbaby."

He was right about that I though. Although his mom seemed nuts to me. My daughter was just as safe in her care as she was in my mother's care.

"Look. I know I fucked up with you. But I'm trying to do right by her. Trust me."

I took a deep breath. "Okay. Just look after my child please. I don't want to be on my trip worrying about her. And remember per the court order you are not to take her from your mother's house."

"You won't. I want to help you co-parent now Allure. I don't want you to have to worry. Sierra told me that all last year you were stressed out. If I can lift some weight off of you take away some the stress I will. Let's start now. I don't want us to fight anymore I want us to get along for Sierra's sake because all her life she has never seen that."

"Greg I want the same thing."

"Okay. Let's start today."

We even hugged it out!

The day we boarded the plane I borded it with no apprehension at all. I actually felt at ease and hopeful for the future that Greg and I could actually co-parent with him. I was having a ball, hitting up the different clubs and trying all the different types of food. I even met a few guys out there. When my trip was over I couldn't wait to get home and see Sierra only I was in for a rude awakening.

I was all smiles when I knocked on Greg's mother's door.

The wooden door was opened but the screen door was closed. I saw a half dressed lady who looked my age on the couch.

Greg came to the door quickly snapped, "Wait by your car!"

I jumped, taken aback by the anger in his voice which was so different from how he sounded just five days ago.

But I walked to my car and waited for him to bring Sierra out.

As I saw them coming my way I got back out of my car excitedly to give her a hug. She didn't look the same though.

"Hey Sierra!" I hugged her and when I pulled back I gasped at what I saw. She was wearing a pair of shorts and a t-shirt. Both were heavily stained and on top of this there were bump after bump covering her legs. Her arms had bites as well.

"What happened to her?" I exclaimed.

"She got bit by a few fleas."

A few fleas? They were completely covering her legs, arms, ankles and feet. I pulled up her shirt and shrieked as I saw more bites all over her chest, and abdomen.

"Wait a minute! What happened to my baby?" I demanded loudly.

He scowled at me and got in my face. "I just told you what the fuck happened!" he said.

I backed up a little. But continued to press, as my eyes scanned her body. Ther was also caked blood on Sierra where it appeared she had scratched the bites so much she had bleed.

"Have you taken her to a doctor?"

"No."

"What about putting ointment on them?"

"No."

"She could get lyme disease! Why would you let this happened to your child and do nothing?"

With fist balled he stepped in my face. "Bitch! You better stop yelling at me!" Spit flew from his mouth into my face as he yelled at me. My heart speeded up because I didn't know if he was going to hit me or not.

I heard someone laughing loudly. I looked towards their apartment and saw the girl that was on the couch *was standing on their porch steps. In that moment I wished to God that I was a man so I could fuck Greg up for allowing this to happen to my child and not care.*

I wiped my tears. "Come on Sierra."

I helped her get in the back seat and snatched on her seatbelt.

As Greg turned to walk away, His mother rushed out of the house, yelling, "I don't want no part of this! He said he was going to take Sierra to the Aquarium and that they would come right back. I called and called him" She pointed at the lady on the porch." I told him not to take that baby to her house. He brought Sierra back with her twat stinking, her hair uncombed and in dirty clothes. Next time you do that I'm calling the police on you!"

"Mom miss me with that bullshit! You always siding with that bitch!" he yelled.

His mom did side with me because she was a mother and she knew all the crap I had to put up with and ho Greg has never been a real father to Sierra. A blind person could see it.

"No I'm not! I'm on the side of right. And there should be no reason why you neglect Sierra the way you do! And you continue to put women in front of your baby!"

"Man it was fleas from a rabbit I bought Sierra damn!"

His mom slapped one of her hands into her free palm. "Plain and simple you don't take good care of your baby!"

Greg tossed a hand at his mother. "Come on baby! Lets go!"

I simply drove away.

I rushed my daughter to the closest hospital. I remember waiting there all day until she was fially seen.

Words could not describe the look of disgust the doctor gave me when he saw all the bites on Sierra.

"How did this happen?"

She was with her dad and she was bit up by fleas."

"Well you know these will all be permanent."

I looked away and nodded. I did'nt want that for my daughter's beautiful brown skin. What if other kids at school made fun of her? That wasn't the only thing on my mind. What if the doctor called Social Services?

The doctor gave me a prescription for her. "This is for the itching. Nothing can be done about the scarring. I've never seen a case so bad." He shook his head in disgust again.

"Thank you," I spit out. My shoulders shook with sobs. I grabbed one of Sierra's hands and we left to get the prescription.

When we got home I ran Sierra a bath, let her soak because she was filthy. Point blank.

After I bathed her I dried her off and rubbed her down with the ointment. For more relief, I gave her a Benadryl. I ordered pizza and as Sierra ate, I couldn't. I was pissed that he could be such a piece of shit father to neglect his daughter this way.

For the safety of my child, I stopped letting him see my child. Eventually, through the courts I was forced to give him monitored visitation and after a year and a half of him cooperating with this, he took me back to court again and just recently was able to have Sierra at his mother's house again for one weekend a month, despite me urging the judge to continue with the monitered visitation. Most of the time Sierra declined to go. Since she was a little older and had a cell phone now I felt a little better but I never completely trusted Greg with my child. But it had been almost three years since that fiasco and nothing

more crazy had happened. But still . . . I mean that was
the crazy part about the system. These sorry ass daddies
were able to get away with fucking murder and still be
able see their kid. Yes I take a responsibility for having
a kid by a piece of shit but still. I grew up. When the fuck
would he grow up and actually do right? Not semi right
but all the way? I'll wait.

To tell the truth, I wasn't really dating anyone. I had
been so focused the first two years on my student teaching and my credential. Then, once I got my credential,
I focused on my first year of teaching. With five classes
equaling 150 students, content standards, and lesson
plans, I was so overwhelmed that I really didn't have the
time to date. That was not to say that I didn't get lonely.
I did, and horny as hell. To solve this, I had invested in
the best BOB, battery-operated boyfriend, I could find.
And I pulled that bad boy out during nights that seemed
unbearable, handled my business, and took my ass right
to sleep. I also knew I simply needed to stay focused and
learn from past mistakes.

And twice a month, I volunteered at the Domestic
Violence Crisis Center in North Long Beach. I did the
intake for a few hours. Cool part was Sierra was able to
come with me. Usually, I counseled the mothers and
helped them with finding shelter and services geared
toward empowering them to leave their abusive partner,
such as counseling, free child care, and financial support.
Usually, if they had a small child, Sierra would entertain
her or him. A lot of times the women went back to their
abusive partner, and a lot of times they didn't. But it felt
good to give back. I was, after all, one of those women.

I dodged another phone call from James as Sierra and
I rushed out of the house to go to church. Truth was, I
hadn't ever gone to church like I should. In the past three

years I hadn't been going. Student teaching and classes had prevented this, because my weekends had been reserved for studying. In the past year I had used Sundays to grade assignments, tests, and papers. But I had a better schedule down now, so there was no excuse for not going.

I drove to North Long Beach, to a church called Artesian Well Faith Center. When Sierra and I got inside, it was packed. Sierra went to children's church, leaving me to go on to the second floor.

The pastor was giving a sermon about being on the brink of a blessing. When my phone went off, people near me exchanged disapproving looks. Kendra was calling me. I pressed IGNORE and put my phone on vibrate. Then I focused on what the pastor was saying. What he was explaining in a nutshell was how to cope in the meantime, while you were on that brink. He said we needed to hold on, stay in prayer, and stay positive.

As he read a passage, which I tried to find on my cell, a text came through from Kendra, telling me to call her.

I texted back, Will hit you back later.

Just when I found the passage the pastor was reading, my phone buzzed again. It was a text from James.

What did that man want? It had been a month since our encounter. Damn! I ignored it and continued to read along silently with the pastor, but then my mind went back to that night we had had sex. What was so crazy to me was the fact that after three years, it had seemed like no real time had passed. Damn, that was not a good thing. Because that meant I was not over him. And James was also still as cocky, smooth, and fine as ever. That made the shit harder. I glanced down at my phone as another text came through. It was also from him.

I didn't read it. Instead, I glanced up and saw people making their way down the stairs. I figured it was offering time. I pulled out my checkbook and a pen. By this time they had all made their way down the stairs, as there weren't many people on the second floor. I made my way down the stairs, filling in the check as I went. I tore it out of my checkbook as my feet touched the last step. Only, the step felt soft, like a blanket covered it. I knew I had done something wrong, because the sound of the band was now super loud in in my ears, like I was on the stage with them. That was because I was on the stage! *Damn. Damn. Damn.*

The singer was in her groove, shouting, "Jesus! Jesus!" Her back was to me, and she was doing her "Lord, hallelujah" dance. A dance that caused her to back right into me and drop the microphone.

Mortified, I quickly picked up the mic and handed it back to her.

"God bless you, sister," she said. And then she went on with her "Jesus! Jesus! Jesus!"

I turned, still mortified, and must have moved too quickly, because I collided with the usher who was holding the collection plate. The money and checks in the collection plate flew around our heads like she had just made it rain in a strip club.

"That's all right, baby. God still loves you!" someone shouted.

The ushers all scrambled to help her pick up the money.

"I'm so sorry," I said. I handed one of the ushers the check I had written.

I walked back toward the stairs with my head down and then went back up the stairs. I realized the mistake I had made was that I picked the wrong set of stairs to go down.

The pastor wiped his forehead, someone played a few keys on the piano, and he said, "See, we all fall down, but we get up. She knocked the usher down, but she got up and gave a donation. Praise God. Say, Sister Jenkins, how much is it for?"

The usher pulled my check out of the collection plate, scanned it, and said, "Fifty dollars, Pastor."

"God bless her."

"Praise God!" someone yelled.

The church then started clapping.

The organ played, and the pastor started doing the pastor dance.

I tried to smile, but I was *so* embarrassed.

The service went from bad to horrific when I drank my grape juice and devoured my cracker too fast. I gave the older usher man a smile as he continued to stare at me and shake his head as everyone held their juice and cracker.

"Did I drink it too soon?" I whispered.

"Did God tell you to do it?"

"No."

"Then yes."

That was all I needed to hear to know that I needed to get out of that church before I caused another catastrophe, and so I did. But this time I went down the right set of stairs.

Chapter 5

Sierra could not stop cracking up when I told her what had happened to me. We were on the way to her basketball game. We had stopped at McDonald's to get her a salad—her coach had said she had to eat light before her game—and I grabbed a Big Mac, fries, and a Coke for myself.

"Ha-ha!"

"Shut up," I told her.

The thing about my relationship with my daughter was that we really had grown up together. I loved how understanding my daughter always was. As life got harder, I found myself being less patient than I'd been when she was small. But she always reassured me that she understood.

She continued laughing and munching on her Caesar salad. "Only you, Mom."

I joined her in her laughter.

Now, I knew I shouldn't let anything or anyone get in the way of my salvation, but the bottom line was that what had just happened was so embarrassing I could not show my face at that church again. No way. I would have to find my salvation somewhere else.

Sierra slipped her earbuds in her ears and turned on the music player on her phone. I had bought her and myself the new Samsung Galaxy S III. The only drawbacks were I ended up changing my number and had to adjust to a touch screen. It drove me crazy. Sierra loved it. It was funny how in three years she went from wanting to be under me and playing with dolls to having her own identity and talking to her friends.

I shook my head and chuckled.

She pulled out her earbuds and asked, "Mom, do you think Daddy will come to my game? I told him I was starting, and he said he would."

"Maybe, Si." But he had already missed the first four games of the season, and she had invited him to those as well. I hoped that ungrateful bastard wouldn't let her down this time. This would be the first time she would start.

"I hope he does. The fathers of all the other girls on the team come to their games."

"I know. Hopefully, he will. But don't get upset if he does not. And when you talk to him next, you tell his ass how you feel."

"Okay." She put her earbuds back in.

Once we made it to the gym, Sierra went to warm up with her team and I settled on one of the benches. I looked around for her dad and didn't see him. Once the game started, he was still a no-show, so even if he did come, which would have been good for Sierra, he would have missed her start. But as the game went on, he still didn't show up. I knew it upset Sierra, and she seemed a little frazzled during the game. Several times she looked into the bleachers like she was looking for him. The distractions left her open and she missed several assists and the ball was stolen from her twice.

Once the game was over and we were on the way to the car, I asked her, "You okay?"

She looked down, and she said in a quiet voice, "He promised me he would come, and he didn't. What's there to talk about? Mom, I don't want to talk about it."

"Okay."

She slipped into the backseat and put her earbuds in. I got in, put on my seat belt, started the car, and drove out of the parking lot to the busy street.

I really felt bad for her and was enraged by his bullshit. Why the hell did the bastard tell her he was going to come to the game if he wasn't? Damn! I tried to concentrate on the road and get my mind off his latest bullshit. Greg sure was a sorry-ass excuse for a father. And he honestly, in his heart, believed he was a great dad. On Father's Day he made sure he dressed up in a suit and a fucking hat, like he was father of the year and shit. He wasn't even father of the second.

My cell phone started ringing, interrupting my thoughts. The caller was Kendra.

I answered it quickly. "Hello?"

"Girl, I have been calling you all week."

"Sorry, girl. I meant to get back to you."

"Look, I got some news for you! Elijah's cousin moved out here from Louisiana a few months ago. Girl, he is thirty-four, single, and guess what he does for a living?"

"Stripper," I joked.

"No, fool. He is a fireman. And he is fine as hell."

Fine, with a job? "How did he manage to stay single?"

"Well, he came out here on a mission. To get a job and a place. He said the next step is a wife."

I sighed. Three years ago I would have been ecstatic about being hooked up. But right now . . . I didn't know. I had been single for three years. No dates, phone calls . . . nothing. I wasn't tripping, in all honesty, and no part of me wanted to jump back in the lying and deceitful dating pool. Being with another man like James, Greg, Lavante, and Bryce scared the shit out of me. I did not want to be hurt ever again.

"Girl, I don't know."

"What? Girl, I'm in love and happy, and I want the same for you. No one deserves to be happy more than you do, Allure. I'm not letting you wait around, so be at my house tomorrow at six. And wear something nice. You got that body in shape, so you better show it off, missy."

I laughed. "Okay. See you tomorrow, girl."

"Bye."

I ended the call and drove down the street where our home was. I glanced in my rearview mirror at Sierra. She still had her earbuds in. I hoped if I cooked something really good for dinner and popped in a movie, it would make her feel better. I glanced in the mirror again and saw a tear slide down one of her cheeks. It tugged at my heart.

I pulled into my driveway. I saw a man standing on my steps. It was James.

I closed my eyes briefly. *What the hell is he doing here?* I thought. I put my car in park.

"Mom! Is that James?"

Before I could respond, Sierra jumped out of the backseat and raced toward him.

He looked up, surprised, and smiled. It was a genuine smile. He opened up his arms to her, and she leaped into them. Though she was a lot bigger than she was three years ago, he lifted her easily. "Hey, baby girl."

I unfastened my seat belt and got out of the car. I grabbed my purse, never taking my eyes off of them. Thing was, this was the main reason I had not brought another man around in the past three years. Kids got attached. It was so easy for a man to leave, to simply pass through, to come into a single mother's life and walk right back out of it, almost as if he hadn't been there at all. Yet the memory of his presence stayed with the kids. And sometimes even with the mother. Men pretended they were there for the long haul, to see what you could build together. But they truly have no real intention of sticking around. Then the mom was left picking up the pieces.

Thing was, Sierra really cared about James. And she had often asked about him after he left. But like me, she had eventually accepted that he was not coming back. During the time James and I were together, he was like a father to her. The sad part was that no matter how much you loved a person and no matter how long you were with a person, things just might not work out. And there was that kid. And in some women's case, those kids. I had grown up watching men come and go in my mother's life. Some I loved; some I hated. But I sought a father's love from every single one of them. They sought nothing from me, but to get the fuck out of their sight so that they could screw my mother.

So the fear of Sierra being hurt again was another reason why I had remained alone.

I walked toward them and heard him tell her, "You getting so big and beautiful." He kissed her on both her cheeks, and she blushed.

I pierced him with a look that said, "What are you doing here?"

"Hey," he said.

I nodded.

Sierra held on to one of his hands. "James, come see my room."

He chuckled and looked at me and shrugged.

I walked up the steps and unlocked the door. They walked past me, Sierra opened the door, and both of them shot inside. I shook my head and went into the kitchen to prepare chicken enchiladas for dinner. I wanted to tell him to get the fuck out. But, damn, James being on our doorstep had wiped the sadness out of Sierra's eyes.

I grabbed the pack of chicken breasts that I had left in the sink to thaw before we went to church. I rinsed the chicken, seasoned it with salt, garlic salt, and pepper, and placed it in a skillet to cook. While it sizzled, I glanced around the kitchen and could hear Sierra laughing loudly. I then opened a can of red enchilada sauce, poured it into a bowl, and added my special ingredients: ketchup, sugar, salt, and pepper. Usually, Sierra would grate the cheese, but I decided to do it. As I turned the chicken over in the pan, James walked into the kitchen.

"Why are you here?" I demanded through clenched teeth.

"Well, babe—"

"Don't play with me, James!"

"I was in the neighborhood, and I was just checking up on you."

"In the neighborhood? James, spare me the corny shit. What are you doing at my house?"

"Look, you were on my mind, that's all."

"Never in my life have I met a man more selfish than you. You have a wife and two kids, and yet you are here again?"

Sierra ran into the kitchen. "Mommy, is it okay if James stays for dinner?"

I gave him an evil look, as he had the nerve to stare at me anxiously, waiting for my response.

"Sierra, I really don't think James can. He needs to go home to his family." I arched a brow when I said the word *family*.

"But, Mom, I haven't seen him in three years. Can he just stay for dinner?" she pleaded.

I looked away. "Okay."

She kissed me on my cheek and turned to James, grabbing one of his hands again. "James, come see my pictures on Facebook!"

He allowed her to pull him back toward her room.

An hour later, we all sat down to eat. It was awkward as hell sitting across from James as he ate my enchiladas, salad, and Spanish rice like he was starving.

Sierra giggled at him. "Dang, James! Did you eat today?"

He covered his mouth with a fist and laughed. "Yes. It's just that I have always loved your mother's cooking. No one I have ever met has been able to top it. Real talk."

"This feels like the old days, huh, Mommy?"

Before I could respond, she looked at James and said, "I think about you all the time, James." Her voice sounded so sad. I looked away.

"I think about you a lot too, baby girl. I missed you."

Her eyes got watery.

"That's it! Get your ass out! Leave, James!" I stood from my seat and stomped out of the kitchen and into my bathroom.

I slammed the door shut and sat on the toilet and cried. My daughter should not have to feel any type of pain because of the men I allowed in my life, so to a huge degree, I blamed myself for this shit. I chose Greg and got pregnant by him. I chose James. I wasn't focused on what they were doing to me, but more so on what they had done to her. The key words were *I chose*. I bore the responsibility for them hurting her. Had I done things differently, we wouldn't be here right now. Sierra used to cry for James after he left us for good. And she would ask for him. But we got past it. Well, sort of. And here he was again, confusing things. Disrupting shit.

When I heard a knock on the bathroom door, I wiped the tears off my face and got up to open it. James was standing behind it.

"Look, I'm sorry for upsetting you. And if you want me to leave, I will. But for the record, I did not come here to start fucking things up. It's just . . . There are times when I wonder about you, how you doing, and I feel I need to check up on you. It's out of concern."

"Where was the concern when you cheated on me, raped me, left me, and married home chick? You felt I could handle all that with ease. You never came around to check on me then, to see how I was doing. I was a big girl, right? But not so much anymore? Now that we are past you, all of a sudden I can't handle life? I *need* you to check up on me? Protect me? James, please."

"You, Allure, are probably the strongest woman I have ever met. But no woman should have to handle the stuff I put you through. It doesn't make you weak if you had a hard time coping with that shit. I'm just saying, pretty often I just want to make sure you two are okay. I was a very selfish man before, but I have changed, even if you don't see it."

"What made you change?"

"My sons."

I started to ask him if Jeremiah had changed him, but I swallowed that question.

"Sierra is my world," I told him. "I love that little girl to a degree I never thought possible. No matter all the shit I had to go through, from sleeping on a staircase with her to washing her clothes out in a motel room, I have a commitment to her beyond all means of comprehension. And it's enough her dad hurts her and lets her down. I do not want another man, new or old, coming in and doing the same thing. And to me, that person is you. So I don't want you coming around here, James. Put your love and time into your own family, and leave what is left of mine alone."

He frowned. "So you won't just give me a chance to prove to—"

"No. Now please get out of my house."

He took a deep breath. "All right. But if you need anything, baby, don't hesitate. Hit me up. You and Sierra."

He turned and walked out of the house.

Still, I was curious as to how James was living. So once Sierra went to sleep, I grabbed her laptop and opened up James's Facebook page. I looked at all his pics of himself, his wife, and his boys. I even read his wall. The day before he had posted, "Congrats to my big bro for finally getting another job. Fuck the haters!" Then, just seconds after he left my house, he posted from his iPhone, "Just saw someone really special. Damn."

I gasped and closed my daughter's laptop. I knew he was talking about me. Maybe he really did love me. I knew I loved him. But nothing could come of it, because like he had said, the fucked-up decisions he made had made things the way they were.

Chapter 6

The next morning, a few minutes before class, I was cleaning off my chalkboard when I heard a knock on my classroom door. I turned around and was surprised as hell when Omar, James's brother, step into my classroom.

As he walked toward me, his expression seemed a lot friendlier than it had during our last encounter, when he told me James had gotten married. He had treated me so coldly and callously on his doorstep when I demanded that James come outside so he could explain to me why he didn't keep his word and come back to talk to me. As much as I wanted to give him attitude, the "Fuck you" finger, or just plain tell him to get the fuck out of my classroom, I knew it wouldn't be professional. So I tried to give him a genuine smile as he made his way over to me.

"Hello, Ms. Jones. I'm the new math teacher."

"Hi, Omar. How are you?" That was what James was talking about on his page. I never would have imagined Omar's uppity ass would work for L.A. Unified. What happened to his physician's assistant job?

"I'm good. It's good to see you. I know the last meeting wasn't a positive one." Omar looked so much like his brother. They had the same features, the same build, but Omar was a few shades lighter than James.

"Well, let's not even focus on that. We have to work together. And I prefer if it is harmonious between the two of us. So let's start over again."

He chuckled and held out his hand. I shook it. "I'm just happy to be working again," he said.

"Oh, trust that if you can handle yourself here, no one will come looking to take your job."

"Yeah. I heard it's pretty rough here. I can't help but feel a little apprehension."

"Change is always hard. But you will adjust, and you will be fine. Despite the school's reputation, we have some great kids here who want to learn and who are extremely bright."

"Okay, I hope so, because they look rather thuggish."

I laughed at him and shook my head. "You sound so snobbish."

"Oh, my bad."

Just then the bell rang.

"See you around," he said as he backed out of the room, still facing me.

I smiled and waved as my first period class piled into the room. I couldn't help but think how small our world was that James's brother would end up working for the same school district that I worked for. I hoped he wouldn't be the messy type and tell all my personal business. The thing about my job was that I was extremely quiet. I had learned from my past jobs not to tell all my personal business. People were unhappy and insecure, so you could never trust their motives for getting in your personal business. All in all, I just thought it was better to keep my personal life personal. I was still friendly, and sometimes I went to the potlucks they had, but I always left it at that. I figured as long as I was nice to Omar, he would play nice as well. Well, I hoped he would.

Creole was kind enough to babysit Sierra for my meeting with Christopher, the guy Kendra had insisted on fixing me up with. It was fall, and since I had to be at Kendra's at 6:00 p.m., I wore a long-sleeved, form fitting black-and-white-striped dress that stopped at my knees and some black suede heels. I also wore a bangle bracelet and some gold hoop earrings, and I sprayed my braids. Yes, I still wore braids. I still wasn't into makeup, so I simply put on some lip gloss and a little clear mascara on my lashes. I sprayed on my Victoria's Secret Strawberries and Champagne perfume, and I was ready to go. Not much had changed about my style, except I now allowed myself to purchase a Michael Kors bag once a year. And I had also upgraded to a nicer car. I drove a 2012 black Honda Accord.

When I arrived at Kendra's house, a part of me was reluctant to get out of my car. In all honesty, I did want to meet someone, but I didn't want to be reintroduced to bullshit. Bullshit was what often came with the men I had encountered. Christopher just might be worse than any man I had been with so far, or maybe he was a combination of all of them, heaven fucking forbid.

My cell phone buzzed, interrupting my thoughts. It was a text message from James. It read, Hey. How are you? I rolled my eyes and shoved my phone back into my purse. James was getting on my damn nerves. Did he really think we were going to be friends?

I saw Kendra come out her front door. I chuckled as she stood there, waving for me to get out of my car. There was obviously no way I was going to be able to get out of this, even if I wanted to. She was all smiles, though, and this calmed me. I unfastened my seat belt, grabbed my purse, and got out of my car. Kendra was walking toward me.

"Hey!" she called. She was so energetic, like I always remembered her to be. And she looked so happy. *Oh, to be in love,* I thought. It was one of the best feelings in the world. Like Sylvia Plath said, "Love set you going like a fat gold watch." But me, I had some serious doubts that I would ever be able to find and claim love. I figured a guy might come around. But really that was all it would ever be. No one would ever really *stick* around. I felt this way because no one ever had. But instead of shooting down my prospects, I could give them a try again, or I would never really know.

"Hey," I said, laughing. "You are just on cloud nine." I gave her a hug.

"Christopher is not here yet. But he texted me and said he is on his way."

I followed after Kendra. She lived in a cozy two-bedroom condo on the east side of Long Beach, while I resided in North Long Beach. I liked that we were not far from each other.

"How is the little one?" I asked.

"Just a cutie. I'm going to take you to him right now."

We walked into her living room, then down the hall to her den. Her husband, Elijah, was sitting on the couch with the baby in his arms.

"Hi, Elijah," I said.

"What's going on, Allure?"

I loved Elijah for my friend. He was a great provider. He was a probation officer, and he was such a Southern gentleman.

"Now, you know I want to hold him. But let me wash my hands first," I announced.

I dashed off to their hallway powder room and washed my hands. I then went back into the den. I sat down next to Elijah, and he gently handed the baby to me.

Holding him . . . I didn't know. It felt so good. I knew babies naturally evoked warm and fuzzy feelings by default. But in addition to this, the baby reminded me of what I was missing in my life. Also, without a doubt, the baby brought me back to Jeremiah. To me, babies represented love . . . God, even.

For some reason, Kendra's eyes got watery. When she caught me staring at her, she wiped them quickly and forced a smile. Just then the doorbell rang.

"I'll get it, baby." Kendra walked out of the den.

"So what you think of my seed, Allure?"

"He's beautiful."

"That's 'cause his Daddy is beautiful," he joked. He took one of his hands and rubbed it down his beard in a quick motion. I busted up laughing. I saw why Kendra had fallen in love with him. I stared down at the fat-cheeked, brown-skinned baby, who smelled so good.

I continued to stare down and coo at the baby until a few moments later, when I heard someone clear their throat. I looked up. Kendra was super cheesing and staring as she stood next to one of the finest men I had ever seen in my life. *Shit,* I thought. This couldn't possibly be who Kendra was hooking me up with. And I just so happened to blurt "Shit" out loud.

Elijah busted up laughing and said, "Allure, you crazy."

Kendra made the introductions. "Allure, this is Christopher. Christopher, my friend Allure."

Elijah gently took the baby out of my arms.

Christopher bent over and clasped one of my hands in his. He held it and hesitated about letting it go when I tried to pull back. I gazed at him again. He was super tall, like six feet three. His shoulders and chest were broad, and his arms were muscular. He was built like a linebacker. He had brown skin and tight eyes. His nose was small and curved at the tip. It was perfect. He had a beautiful smile. And I was trying my damnedest not to drool. He was dressed casually but, thank God, not like a thug. He wore a black button-down top with a pair of fitted jeans and a pair of Jordans. And he smelled so, so good. I tried to keep a look of lust off my face. He stared at me, letting his eyes rake up and down my body and face.

For a moment I forgot about Elijah and Kendra, until she said, "So what do you think about my friend?"

Without hesitation he said, "That she is beautiful." His voice was deep and husky. I could head the Southern accent. And as he talked, he would not stop looking at me.

I blushed and looked away.

Elijah got up with the baby, leaving Christopher to take the seat next to me.

"Chris, remember I was telling you that Allure has a daughter that is just as pretty as she is?" Kendra said.

"I do. I love kids."

That was when Elijah said, "Baby, leave them alone so they can chop it up."

"Okay, baby." Kendra winked at me and followed Elijah out of the room.

Christopher bit his lip, chuckled, and said, "I know these first meetings can be a little awkward."

I nodded. "They can be."

"So how was your day?"

"It was pretty good. But my days are always crazy with teaching. But the day always manages to fly by."

"You like teaching?"

"I love it. I really couldn't imagine doing anything else, honestly. How about you?"

"Oh, I feel the same. Career-wise, I'm right where I want to be. I'm just lacking in other areas of my life."

"Like?"

"Well, in all honesty, I want a nice, sweet lady in my life." He looked away and added, "You going to help me out there?"

I laughed. "Are you sure about that? Because men say that all the time."

"Well, for one, I'm not from here. And for two, anything I say, I'm genuine. What else is there to do once you grow up then have a wife and a family? The club or chasing after women? That gets old really fast. I don't have the time for that. At the end of the day, when I leave this world, it is not going to matter how many women I have bedded. And you break a lot of hearts trying to be a player. I went to college, so I been there and done that, and it is definitely out of my system, Allure. Trust me."

Although I listened to him, a part of me was super skeptical. Men said this shit all the time. Granted, it didn't sound as eloquent as he had put it, but it didn't mean shit. After all, he could just be talking to get up under my skin and in my panties. My experience had taught me not to take everything a man said for face value. I had done that too many times before. He would simply have to show me. Nevertheless, I enjoyed being around him and having a conversation with him. Christopher was a cool person to talk to, even if that was all he would be to me. And the chemistry was off the chain.

Chapter 7

The next day, after work, I got another surprise. As I sat down to watch Sierra play at one of her games, James walked into the gym and paused in the doorway, scanning the bleachers until he saw me. He smiled at me. I didn't smile back. He made his way over to me.

What the hell is his ass doing here? I thought. This fool was really not going to let up. Why was he continuing to come around?

He sat down next to me.

"Hey, baby."

I frowned at the "baby" comment. "Why are you here?" I asked tersely.

"Sierra texted me and asked me to come. I didn't have any plans, so I told her I would come."

I was immediately hit with apprehension. I knew why Sierra had invited him. She must have pretty much given up on the possibility of her dad coming through. Maybe she had more faith in James than in her daddy. And I couldn't be mad at James, because at the end of the day, he came through for her, regardless of his intentions. Even if he did it for me, it would still make her day. So I appreciated him coming, and I couldn't be mad at Sierra for inviting him, especially since her teammates' dads were constantly there. Sierra deserved the same.

Just then Sierra made a basket. James and I both cheered.

"Go on now, baby girl!" he yelled.

I chuckled as James and I clapped for Sierra. "Watch them elbows, twenty-four. Get off baby," he shouted, looking annoyed when a player Sierra was trying to block elbowed her.

I laughed louder as he continued to yell out.

"Man, Ref. Call the fouls!"

"James, shhh."

He winked at me.

Despite the fact that James had not been around for the past three years, I had to admit he was really focused on the game.

"You know your brother works at my school?"

"Yeah, he told me. He saw you. I'm just happy he is working again."

I thought he was a doctor."

"Well, he got caught up in some medical malpractice bullshit. He won't tell me the real. He could easily get some dough from my parents, but he doesn't want to tell them. Thus he is teaching."

"James, for the sake of me keeping the peace at my job, please do not discuss me with your brother. Okay?"

He looked in my eyes. "I won't. On my kids. Real talk."

"Thank you."

"Go ahead, Sierra!" he yelled.

She had just made a basket. I laughed and clapped alongside him.

A couple times during the game, I saw Sierra glance up at us. She ended up scoring seven points that game.

"That's the most she has ever scored," I said when the game was over.

"That's because I've been giving her tips. Has her father been coming to her games, practices, or anything?"

"No. He always promises her he'll be here, but he never comes through."

"Why does he keep letting her down like that?"

I had to agree. Greg had been doing that since she was born, being really selfish with his money, putting it into himself, leaving me to buy the things she needed. And he had never spent time with her when we were together, much less now. In the past three years he had become even worse. Months and months would go by and she wouldn't even hear from him. He played a cold game when it came to being a father.

"Well, we both know that Greg has never been the best father. But don't forget that after Jeremiah died, you dropped us both like hot potatoes. Surely, you have to know that that had an effect on her as well."

The self-righteous look he had had when he put down Greg vanished and was replaced with a guilty look. He looked away and didn't speak anymore.

Sierra was in such good spirits after the game.

"You were playing that defense, Sierra," James told her. Of course, he had to walk us to our car. "Sierra, I know a game to help you with your free throws. Here is what you do." As he continued to talk, my cell rang.

It was Christopher. I answered the phone with a little smile, happy to hear from him.

"Hello?"

"Hey, babe. I feel special that you answered my call. I thought my country ass had scared you away."

I laughed, catching James's attention. He turned and looked at me but kept talking to Sierra. I noticed that he kept his eyes on me. I ignored him.

"No. You definitely didn't scare me away."

James got quiet as we reached my car. I unlocked the doors.

"So what are you doing, beautiful?" Christopher asked.

I blushed at the "beautiful" comment. "I'm just leaving my daughter's game."

Sierra hopped in the back.

"Did she win?"

"She sure did."

I glanced at James. At this point, Sierra was safely in the car, so there was really no need for him to stick around, but his ass did. And I didn't feel comfortable talking to Christopher in front of James. If James really did still care for me, I didn't want to do him like that, even if he had done me that way.

"Christopher, let me give you a call back."

"Okay, baby."

"Bye."

I looked at James as I opened my car door. I knew he wanted to ask me who the guy was. It was all over his face. But he didn't.

He simply said, "Drive safe."

"Thank you." I got in my car and didn't bother to look his way again.

I picked some Panda Express up for Sierra and myself, and we drove over to the center so I could do a couple hours. It was a twenty-four-hour business, and you never knew when a woman would pop in.

When we walked in, I saw Jan, the owner. She was a black woman who was in her late sixties. She had been running the center for the last fifteen years. Her daughter was killed by her husband, who had been abusing her daughter since they got married, and Jan never, ever knew. While she had plenty of volunteers who performed different functions, Jan loved to use me for one-on-one crisis counseling. The reason was that I was once an abused woman, so they often related to me, and I was pretty good at persuading the women to sign up for services. The organization was nonprofit. We offered a temporary emergency shelter for the night. And within twenty-four hours, we found the women who agreed to sign up, shelter in a different city so they could get away from the abusive partner. And if they went to the shelter, they were eligible to get emergency Section 8.

The ultimate goal was to get them away from the abusive partner before they were killed, or before they cracked and killed their partner and ended up in prison. The thing that amazed me about volunteering there was that I met women from all walks of life. Young, old, black, white, Asian, Hispanic. Women on welfare, women with degrees. Women who were successful, and women who were not yet established. Domestic abuse crossed all cultural and economic lines. It was crazy to me. The woman you least expected to see and interact with on a daily basis, whose life you thought was so perfect, was going home and getting her ass beat. And you would never know.

"Hey, ladies," Jan said.

"Hi," Sierra, said.

"Hi, Jan."

I looked around. There was one other worker there. She was taking the calls at one of the desks. She smiled and nodded at me. I smiled and waved.

Jan walked up and gave me a hug. She then hugged Sierra. "Allure, I'm so glad you came in today. I have someone back there who specifically requested to talk to you. She is in the back room."

I turned to Sierra and pointed a finger. "Get your homework done, missy."

Sierra nodded, pulled up to an empty desk, and un-zipped her backpack.

I walked to the back room. It was where the counseling sessions were held. There were couches, toys, and a TV in the room, so if the woman had a child, the child had something to do.

I closed the door, looked around the room, and saw a young black girl sitting on a couch, rocking a small child in her arms. The girl looked really young, like nineteen or twenty. And her daughter was adorable. I couldn't stop staring at her daughter. But it wasn't just because she was adorable. I had met so many adorable children since I had been volunteering there. The reason I couldn't stop looking at her was that she reminded me so much of Sierra when she was younger. She had the same brown skin, slanted eyes, button nose, and thick hair. And I'd be damned if her mother didn't have her hair in two puff balls, like I used to put Sierra's hair in. At that moment, she was sleep in her mother's arms.

"Hi." I sat in the chair across from her. "I'm Allure."

"Hi," she mumbled.

The whole right side of her face was swollen. I knew how that felt. I had had that happen to me before. My sister had needed me to be a hair model for a hair show. Initially, James had said it was okay. But the day of the show he threw a bitch fit about me going. He ended up slapping me so hard on the side of my face that it was so swollen that it looked like I had two ears. It took weeks and weeks for it to heal. I should have left him then, but I didn't.

"Would you like an ice pack?"

"Naw. I'm cool. My friend Nay Nay came here last year, and she said you helped her out. She told me that when she came, you didn't treat her like a piece of shit, like the pigs do."

"Yes, I remember Nay Nay. She was a sweet girl."

"She said you could help me too. But I don't know how much you can do to convince me, since you didn't convince her, and the last time I heard from her, she'd gone back to her dude and they'd moved away. I ain't heard from her since. "

I wondered how much she knew about Nay Nay and her situation, but truthfully, it really didn't matter. That was her life, and this young lady had her own to live, so I focused on her. "I can if you let me."

She was silent.

"Who hit you?"

"Her daddy."

"Okay, and do you want to leave him?"

"I do. But I have no money and . . ." She started crying.

"It's okay. We can help you with all of that here."

"How?"

"We can get you away from the person who is abusing you. To a different city, so he can't find you. But you have to take the first step."

"Yeah? And what's that?"

"You have to leave him and get a restraining order against him."

"It's her father! How am I supposed to keep her from her daddy! To be honest, if I hadn't . . ."

I nodded. "I know what you are thinking. I been there. You are feeling like this is all your fault. I promise you it's not. And you assume the guilt about her dad not being in her life. But in all actuality, it is unhealthy for him to be around your daughter when he is putting his hands on you. It is an unsafe environment for your child to grow up in. I know firsthand. Trust me—"

"How the fuck would you know? You just work here. You don't know what I been through. You ever been hit? You ever been raped?"

I looked in her eyes and said, "Yes. All of the above. Been homeless. I went through it all. But you know when I said, 'Enough is enough'?"

"When?"

2007 . . .

It was freezing cold as Sierra and I waited on the bus to go home. It was a Tuesday night. I had got out of school at ten, and then I had gone to my mother's house to pick up Sierra because Greg had not bothered to get her. The walk to the bus stop from my mother's house was six blocks down to Redondo Street. Since Sierra was asleep, I carried her in my arms. The problem was, it was like walking down a hill. And it was late. I didn't have Sierra's car seat, and I had never put her in a car without one. We then waited for the bus. Since it was late, the buses usually ran slower. But this bus was way late. By twenty minutes. When it finally came, I breathed a sigh of relief. We got on and found an empty seat. I hoped that when I got home, Greg didn't trip.

When it was our stop at Mahanna Street, I pressed the bell and waited for the bus to stop. Once it did, I carried Sierra off the bus. We had about a block to walk to our apartment. Once I got to our apartment, I opened the bottom door, nearly tripping on Sierra's inflated swimming pool, which sat on the bottom step. I stepped over it and walked up the steps to our apartment, not bothering to close the bottom door. I stood on the top step and balanced Sierra in one arm while I unlocked the door with the other. But before I could open the door, I noticed it was chained. I sighed and banged on the door.

"What the fuck you banging for?" Greg demanded.

I took a deep breath and tried to stay calm. "Greg, it's late, and Sierra is asleep. Please let me lay her down."

He opened the door a slit and looked at me hatefully. "Why the fuck you so late coming back, huh? Where the fuck you been?"

"I went to school, and then I got Sierra. The bus was a little late."

"Don't give me that bullshit!" He slammed the door shut and refused to unchain it. I knew it made no sense to argue with him. He believed what he believed. Jesus himself couldn't come down and convince him otherwise.

Still, for the sake of Sierra, I knocked again. "Can you please let me in?"

I was ignored. Still, I knocked again.

I had no choice but to slip off my coat with my free hand, lay it on the top step, and lay Sierra on top of it. I placed the edges of my coat over her. I then sat scrunched on the step below her. I was forced to stay out there for over an hour. Thing about Greg was that he always assumed that I was with another man.

Then Greg finally unchained the door and let us in. He sat on the living room couch, and I walked into our bedroom. I didn't bother saying anything to him. I didn't bother arguing with him. I was just happy he had let us come inside.

I laid Sierra in her crib, pulled off my clothes, leaving on my bra and underwear. I was too tired to put on pajamas. I crashed in our bed, hoping he didn't start any more drama with me that night.

A few minutes later I felt sleep take over. But that sleep was short lived, as Greg soon crawled in the bed and started rubbing and kissing on me. I was still pissed that he had locked us out, and I was also exhausted, so I told him, "Greg, stop. Let me sleep."

But he wouldn't stop. He unsnapped my bra and started rubbing on my breasts. And I didn't want him to. He then slipped off my panties. His touch was repulsing me because he treated me so badly. I pulled away from him and scooted toward the edge of the bed.

"Oh, like that?"

"I told you I'm sleepy."

"So you don't want me on you?"

I ignored him and curled up in a knot. I had pretty much told him I was tired. Damn.

"Just tell me you don't want me, and I will leave you alone."

I was still silent.

"Allure! Say it!"

"I don't want you," I said.

"Okay."

Before I could stop him, he grabbed me by my hair and dragged me out of the bed to the living room and then out the front door. I screamed all the way. "Greg, please stop!" But he didn't until he'd dumped me on the steps. Then he went back inside and chained the door. I started crying and looked down. The bottom door was open, and whoever walked by would see me naked. Sierra's inflated swimming pool was still on the bottom step. I had two choices: I could either stay where I was on the top step and risk someone walking by and seeing me naked or I could walk down the steps and risk them seeing me but get the swimming pool, cover myself up with it, and close that door.

I decided to walk down the steps and get the pool. I did so quickly, wrapping the plastic pool around my naked body and closing the bottom door. I then walked back up the steps. I crouched on the top step, where I had previously laid Sierra. I found comfort in the fact that Sierra was at least comfortable in her bed. I was out there so long that I dozed off. I woke up when I heard Greg unchain the door. He opened it and pulled me inside by my arms. I didn't fight him, because my body was so cramped, I could barely walk. He shoved me on the couch and got on top of me. When he parted my legs, I protested, "Greg, please stop! I don't want to!"

He ignored my protests and my fighting. He held me down and forced himself inside of me. At this point I gave up fighting and lay there, limp, as he raped me. But while he was getting sensations out of this, I was getting none. As he pumped into me, he said, "You wet. Must be another nigga's cum."

I turned my face away from him and started sobbing. After he unloaded into me, he pushed me away, and I continued to cry.

"Hello? Hello? Are you going to answer my question?"

I refocused on the girl in front of me. "Yes. The reason why I understand more than you know is that I once was you. Now, I know this is hard, but it is something you are going to have to do if you love that girl in your arms. I can guarantee that if you stay, she will be with a man just like him, providing that social services don't take her away."

She looked alarmed when I said that. Then she started crying again. "I don't know how I got myself caught up in a situation like this."

"Easy. Something in our head just never clicked. There are just some things that are automatic deal breakers in a relationship. In a marriage. Abuse is a top one. There should have been something wired in our heads to know that once a man puts his hands on us, that is it. There is no room for reconciling or for second chances. But there is no such wiring. Maybe because we saw our mothers get hit, and when they accepted it, we did as well. Or maybe our self-esteem was so bad that we felt that either we deserved this or we could find no other man to do any different. No matter the reason, you are going to have to break away. I broke away for my daughter so she didn't have to grow up seeing her father beat on me like my father beat on my mother. So she wouldn't feel it was an accepted practice. Like my mother did, because of what she saw her own father do to her mother."

Her mouth was wide at all I had just said.

"You have to do this for her," I told her.

She chuckled. "I thought you were just going to come in here and read something out of a pamphlet and then move on to the next victim."

"No. I was you. And if you let me, all of this can be who you *were*. But you are going to have to make that choice. I tell you, no one can do this but you. I can guarantee that if you don't make the right decision, you will lose her. And anything that is a threat to the livelihood of your kid needs to go. I'm such a better person for leaving."

"And how is your life?"

"I'm a schoolteacher, I recently bought a home for my daughter, and we are happy. Everything I always wanted, I have." Except a husband. But a part of me felt that that was on the horizon.

"Seems like when I had my daughter, my dreams went out the window."

"Well, they don't have to. A child can slow you down, but they won't stop you. Only one person can stop you, and that is yourself. You can still dream big. Now you got some decisions to make. I can find you a place to go tonight. Think on it, and when you decide, I'll be in the front office. When you decide, just pick up the phone and dial three-one-six."

I stood and walked toward the door. Then I stopped and turned around.

"There is one more thing I want to tell you. Nay Nay did go back to her boyfriend. They moved to Moreno Valley. He charmed her with this house he bought out there. She called and told me. And about a month later, she died from a head injury. That's probably why you never heard from her again."

Her eyes widened and she gasped when I said that.

I then left the room.

I found out that the girl was young, only nineteen, her daughter was two, and she had no real family. Her mother was on drugs and cared less about her and more about her next high. She had never met her father. In a sense she was stuck because she and her boyfriend had a place together in Long Beach. We were able to find her a shelter in San Pedro that would take her daughter that night. Sierra and I dropped her off there to ensure that she went.

Once we got to the shelter, Sierra and I went inside and helped her with her referral form and walked her to her room. The process normally didn't take a long time, and the cool part about this shelter in particular was that there were rooms, not just beds. Each room was almost the size of a studio apartment. And after staying there for a few months, the mothers were eligible for emergency housing. I had brought her and her daughter Subway sandwiches, so they sat down to eat.

While they ate, Sierra and I ran over to the ninety-nine cents store across the street from the shelter and bought some toiletries, drinks, and snacks for her and her daughter. When we came back, she had turned on cartoons for her daughter. I placed the bags on the table, along with some bus tokens, food coupons, five twenties, and a crisis center business card with my cell.

"If you need anything else, have any questions, call the office. You know it's open twenty-four hours a day, and here is my cell. Feel free to give me a call."

"Thank you, Allure."

"Bye," her daughter chirped.

"Bye, sweetie."

I was so relieved she was going to give it a chance. But there was always a chance that she would go back to her boyfriend. Most of the time they did. Still, I never let that discourage me from trying to help them. I had gone back to Greg several times, but when I was done, I was done. I just hoped she was done. And if she wasn't, and she went back and then decided to come back down to the office, I would help her again. But I prayed she stayed at the shelter.

Chapter 8

The next day I sat in my classroom and munched on a sandwich while I graded some class work. Instead of going out for lunch, I usually brought my own and ate in my classroom, using that forty-five minutes to my benefit, so that I would have less to do when I got off. Also, some of my students from various periods tended to trickle in and eat their lunch with me. Some read a book or did schoolwork assigned in my class or other classes.

I was surprised when Omar walked into my class.

"Hey," he said with a smile as he walked toward me.

"Hi. How are you doing?"

He pulled a chair up to my desk and sat down. He scanned the classroom and mumbled, "Damn. You just can't get a break from them. Don't they have somewhere else to go?"

I took a deep breath so I didn't go off on him. "I don't mind. It's not taking anything away from me by having them here."

"Well, not me. I need a break from those ghetto bastards."

"The worst kinds of things tend to trickle out of your mouth, don't they?"

He shrugged. "I just speak my mind, is all."

"You know, you're funny to me. You were the one who was out of a job and needed one, yet you are turning your nose down at my kids? It's a little offensive."

"Sierra is yours."

"With a mentality like that, you won't last here. I came from the same struggle these kids come from, and I grew to have struggles of my own as a young mother. Many of them have young mothers. They are every bit as much of me as I am of them."

"I guess I never looked at it like that, *Mr. Clark*." I gave him a weird look, and he held his hands up. "I'm just kidding. And I will try to keep an open mind."

I continued to stare him down.

"I'm sorry. Didn't mean to offend you, Allure. I didn't know you felt so passionately about it. I thought it was just a job to you."

"Well, it's not. Look, at the end of the day you can do whatever you want. But if I were you, I would eat a couple slices of humble pie and understand that this might not be Newport Beach, but we have some very intelligent kids who actually want to learn, despite what you heard or thought about inner city kids. And when you are around me, kindly stop with the negativity, or you will be subject to getting shut down every time."

He held his hands up, as if in surrender. "Okay. I will, real talk."

"All right." I relaxed my face. "So what's up?"

"I came by to see if you could help me out with my lesson plans. They are a pain in the ass to get done."

I laughed. "I had the same problem when I first started. I wanted to pull my hair out. But once I followed the guidelines, I was cool."

"What guidelines?"

"Well, the content standards. Let me show you." I pulled out the lesson plan I had used the day before. "Here is an example for you."

I watched his eyes skim over it. Then I showed him my lesson plan for today. "You'll notice that I keep them consistently the same. And I have had no real issues since I have been doing this."

"Can I keep this?"

"No. But I will make you a copy. I keep all my lesson plans, and I file them." I walked over to my copy machine and photocopied the lesson plan. I then handed the copy to him.

He stood to his feet. "Thank you, Allure."

"You're welcome." I smiled and sat back down at my desk and resumed eating my lunch.

"You know, given what happened with my brother, I really didn't think you and I were going to get along."

I waved a hand and said, "I'm past that."

"Are you?" He looked skeptical.

I narrowed my eyes at him. "It was three years ago, Omar. Sierra and I are good. We are blessed, and I refuse to hold on to baggage."

"Well, that's good. See you later." He walked to the door, turned around, and added, "You know, there is a good spirit about you."

I blushed at that. I knew I was twenty-nine years old, and still, compliments made me blush. The reason why was that growing up, I had never heard them enough. I more often heard what was wrong with me, not what was right. Made me constantly find good things to tell Sierra.

He caught it, chuckled, and walked out of my classroom.

"Damn, he was all in your shit, Ms. Jones. That nigga didn't want no lesson plan."

I held in a laugh at Kenny, one of my students. "Watch your mouth and stay in a teen's place," I said calmly but sternly.

"My bad, Ms. Jones."

When my last period let out, I was relieved and happy it was Friday. Since Sierra was with her daddy, I had

planned on going out with Creole to Grand Lux Cafe.
Then, on Saturday, I was going out with Christopher.

As I hit the freeway, I was surprised to get a call from
Greg. He had Sierra for the weekend.

"Hello?"

"Allure! I got a problem. You and me both."

"What?"

"Angel kidnapped Sierra."

I almost hit the car in front of me. I was instantly struck
with panic. "What!"

"Calm down!"

"Don't tell me to fucking calm down!" I raged. "Where
the fuck is my child?"

"I don't know. I called the police already. My mom said
she came over and took Sierra at gunpoint."

"So that means you have been messing with her again,
haven't you?" After the last fiasco with Angel, where she
whipped my daughter and then I beat Angel's ass, Greg
had promised me that she was out of his life. But appar-
ently, she wasn't. As a matter of fact, the last time I drilled
him on her, he said she had gone back to her country. He
was such a lying piece of shit.

"Allure . . ."

"Answer me!"

"Yes. From time to time. "

Tears clouded my vision, and my heart thudded in my
chest.

"Anyway, I made a police report. They just left."

"Why would she take—"

"'Cause she found out I was fucking with another chick,
and it is her way of getting back at me."

"How the fuck could you let this happen?"

"Don't yell at me, bitch! Just get the fuck over here."

I ignored his insult as dread consumed me. As I drove
to Greg's mother's house, my mind went over how in the

hell this could have happened. Greg had been telling me he was done with her ever since we found out she had beaten Sierra. I hit my thigh in anger. My daughter could very well be severely hurt or killed by this dumb bitch. As I drove, I dialed Sierra's cell but got no answer. It just rang.

"Fuck! Fuck! Fuck!" One of my fists hit the steering wheel. "Dear God, please don't let her hurt my child!" I begged fearfully.

What if she tried to kill her? She had a gun, for God's sake. I sped on the freeway en route to Greg's place.

When I arrived at his apartment, I saw him pacing outside with a cigarette in his mouth. He looked up at me as I parked.

"Where are the police?" I demanded.

"They just left. They took the report and said they would be on it and they would keep in contact with me. And they said if I heard anything to call 'em."

Greg's mom came outside. "Yeah, Allure, that girl is crazy. I told him not to mess with her from the beginning. She came in here with a gun and pulled Sierra out of here!"

I closed my eyes briefly. "Do you know where she could be?"

"No. If I fucking did, don't you think I would have gone there?" he yelled.

"Don't yell at me!" I stormed away from him. "This is your fucking fault." I broke down crying in the street.

His mother walked back into her apartment.

I felt so lost. I pulled out my cell phone and called Creole. I told her what had happened, and she agreed to meet me at Greg and his mother's house. My mother didn't answer, but Kendra did. She agreed to come as well. I called the police and found myself on hold. I wanted to throw my phone. I even put a post on Facebook, hoping if someone saw my baby, they would call the police.

Creole pulled up, parked, and hopped out of her car.
"Allure! What happened?"

I was too choked up to talk.

"I know you didn't call that crazy bitch over to my crib,
Allure," Greg yelled, coming our way.

"Shut the fuck up, you loser!" Creole yelled.

"Bitch!"

"Illiterate bastard. I heard when you was locked up,
someone stuck a finger in your oatmeal and up your
asshole. You flamer."

When he tried to rush toward her, she pulled out a
bottle of what looked like pepper spray. He paused in
mid-step.

My phone started ringing. Frantically, I looked at it. It
was James. I ignored it. Seconds after his call, he sent a
text. I ignored it as well.

"Come on, bitch! I'll blind the fuck out of you with this
wasp spray."

Greg's mother must have heard the commotion, because
she rushed outside. "Greg! Stop this!"

Greg backed away and tossed a hand at Creole.

Creole put her spray back in her pocket and turned to
me. "Did you put it on Facebook?"

I nodded.

"Put it on my page too."

I shared what had happened to Sierra on Creole's page.
I was about to close Facebook but thought better of it.
I could share the terrible news on Sierra's page as well.
Maybe one of her friends would see it. The more people
who knew, the better. But when I went to her page, I
gasped. Sierra had written a frantic message on her wall.

"I been kidnapped. I'm at the L.A. airport!"

My heart started pounding. *Thank God!*

"I know where she is!" I yelled.

"Well, come on. I'll drive," Creole said.

I jumped in Creole's car, and Greg jumped in his. We drove away quickly.

On the way to the airport, I called the detective who had come out and taken the report on Sierra and informed him that she was at the L.A. airport. By the time we got there, the police already had that crazy bitch in handcuffs in the back of a squad car. Kendra and her husband came to the airport as well. The paramedics had Sierra resting in their ambulance. Luckily, my poor baby was okay. I hugged and kissed her like never before, so grateful that she was safe and that crazy bitch wasn't successful in taking her out of the country. The crazy cunt was actually going to take Sierra back to her own country.

Man, I wished I could have whipped her ass again. Because it seemed she didn't learn the first time not to fuck with my child. But surely, they were going to give her punk ass some time for kidnapping. I shook my head as the police drove away with her. The paramedics said that Sierra was pretty shaken up, but she had managed to calm down. I kept my arm wrapped around her as we walked to the car.

When we made it to my car, Greg pulled her away from me, gave her a hug and a kiss.

"Poor Sierra," Creole said. "It's going to take some hot-ass water to get your nappy cooties off of her."

"Fuck you, you bitch!" Greg yelled.

"Hey, man, watch your fucking mouth!"

I looked up, surprised to see James walking up to us at a quick pace.

Greg frowned but kept quiet.

"James!" Sierra pulled away from her dad and ran to James, throwing herself in his arms. I could hear her little sniffles.

"It's okay, baby." James hugged her and kissed her on her cheek.

Greg looked away.

James rubbed his hands up and down her back. He kissed her on her cheek again and said, "Go to your mother."

Greg looked shaken up and started walking away.

I unlocked the door to my car so Sierra could get in. I watched Sierra lie down on the backseat. Kendra and her husband stood near my car.

"Allure, stop James now. I'll wait here," Kendra said suddenly.

All I could say was, "Huh?"

Then Creole and I looked up at the same time and saw that James was following Greg. We both chased after him.

"James, stop!" I ordered.

He ignored me. Greg stopped walking and turned around to face James. James stepped to Greg.

"You know what? I'm not perfect. But you . . . you ain't shit. I been wanting to tell you that for a long time," James snarled.

Greg chuckled nervously. Then, out of nowhere, he attempted to spit on James. James held up his palm in time to avoid getting hit by the saliva.

"That's bitch shit, what you just did, partna. You have a history of doing bitch shit," James growled.

I grabbed James's arm and tried to pull him away.

"Move, Allure." James yanked his arm out of my grasp and turned back to Greg. "You know what else?" he said.

"What, nigga?" Greg tried to act tough.

"This." Out of nowhere James reached back and knocked the shit out of Greg with his closed fist.

Greg fell to the ground.

"Allure forgave you. I didn't. I always wanted to do that shit."

Creole started running around Greg, shouting, "TKO! TKO!"

"James! Stop it!" I yelled, shoving him as he went toward Greg again.

James complied and turned to me. "I apologize, baby. But that sorry-ass nigga deserved that shit."

I shoved him again. "Go! Leave."

Greg attempted to stand to his feet and fell down again. James slowly walked away. As I watched Greg lying there, helpless, it reminded me of all the times he had left me lying somewhere in pain and in tears. He had never shown me any sympathy. Now, while I didn't want Greg to get assaulted by James, I had to admit he did deserve it. And while I wasn't going to sit there and let James beat Greg up, I wasn't going to nurse Greg's wounds, either.

So Creole and I left Greg exactly where his ass was.

Chapter 9

I was so happy to have my daughter back. Angel was a psycho bitch. How dare she even think of kidnapping someone's child? And Greg had been sneaking around with her again, after he promised me they were done. The way it was finally explained to me in a stupid, psychotic-ass two-hour-long conversation with his mother was that Angel had told Greg not to have any further contact with me or Sierra. And if he did, she was going to fuck up his and my world. And she was right. Taking my baby out of the country would have positively ruined my entire life. I thanked God over and over again that I had got my child back and that she was okay. Greg sure knew how to lie.

The night I brought her back home, James called and called. Well, not just him. Christopher was blowing me up also. But I had no energy to talk to either one of them. And I was mad that James had hit Greg. Luckily, Sierra didn't see this. But what if she had? I had tried to shield her from any type of violence, and James knew this. So I turned off my phone and stayed with my daughter. She slept in my bed. And that was fine by me.

By Monday everything was back to normal. When I asked Sierra if she wanted to go to school, she said she was feeling up to going, so I went to work.

When I got to my classroom, I saw Omar standing outside of it.

I greeted him with a smile. "Morning."

"Hey." He had two Starbucks cups in his hands. "I thought about you and bought you a some coffee."

"Aww. Thank you." I grabbed one of the cups and then turned to unlock my room. Once it was open, I stepped inside. He followed after me. I flicked on the lights, then walked over to my desk and sat my stuff down. When I looked up, I saw Omar studying me.

"Not to be an asshole or anything, even though I know I can be, but you look really fatigued. So I'm glad I got that for you."

I chuckled. If he knew what I had just gone through this weekend . . . But I had no intention of telling him my personal business. And I hoped James wouldn't tell him, either. I hoped he'd keep his word.

"So, anyhow, I wanted to tell you the lesson plan you gave me really helped me and made things easier. So I wanted to thank you again."

"No problem. Anytime you need my help with anything, let me know."

He studied me for a moment and chuckled. "You know, sometimes when I pass by, I see how you are with your students. You really seem to like them. And they love you." It was a nice statement, but he managed to fuck it up when he added, "I thought it was all for show. But you really seem genuine to me now."

He really was an asshole. And did he think he was doing me a favor? It was like he was letting me know I now had his approval. So? And? He was James times three.

"Has anyone ever told you that you come off as an asshole?"

"All the time."

I chuckled.

"Am I that bad?"

"Yes!"

"But I brought you coffee. Can a brotha get credit for that?"

I shook my head. "See? You just don't stop."

"Okay. Let's get off me. How are things going in your life?"

"Everything is good. My kid is well. I love my house and, as you have observed, my job."

"Okay. Not missing anything?"

Before I could respond, the bell rang and my students instantly piled into my classroom. I was glad, because he was asking shit I didn't want to answer. I didn't have a problem with Omar, but he was too damn observant of me. *Why? Why the curiosity?* I wondered if he was trying to get info to take back to James.

"We will finish this conversation later," he said.

"I'd rather not," I said in a distracted tone.

And sure enough, as I sat down to enjoy my lunch in my classroom, he came in with his lunch. *Ugh,* I thought. I was fine just with eating and texting back and forth with Christopher, who had asked me out on a date. I had called him on Sunday night and had smoothed things over with him by telling him that Sierra had a forty-eight-hour bug and that was why I wasn't returning his calls. He seemed to believe me.

"Hey," Omar said. He pulled a chair up to my desk.

"Hey."

"Are you busy?"

"No." But mostly I wished he would leave me alone.

"Now, I wanted to finish the convo we were having earlier."

"Do we have to?"

He laughed, looking handsome and reminding me of his brother. "Okay. I'm just curious. Because recently I had a very interesting experience. So I really want to know how it is to date and have a kid."

Oh Lord, I thought.

"I ask this because recently I met a beautiful woman. She has this nice energy about her. And I love the way she carries herself. And, man, is the sexual attraction there. But . . . she has a kid."

"And this is bad because?"

"I don't want to take care of no one else's kids. I feel like most sistas screw up and have kids with losers, and then they decide they want a good man, but the good man is supposed to accept all her baggage? I don't want to take care of someone else's kids. But I love black women. And most of them have kids, so it's like, what's a brotha to do?"

He was infuriating me by the goddamned second. I took a deep, deep breath. "Maybe we do. I take full responsibility for having a baby, who I love to death, with a loser. . . . And I'm sure some other sistas have done the same. Now what? Should we be punished for the rest of our lives because of who we procreated with? Should we not be worthy of love from a good man? And does it make us any less of a good woman?"

"Well, I wasn't talking about you. I—"

"I'm in the same category. Granted, at the age of eighteen and him being twenty two, I didn't get a chance to see what type of Dad he would be until Sierra was born. So while many women procreate with men they know are losers, just as many don't know this. You have many men who think that when the marriage or relationship ends, so does their relationship with their kids. What I believe is nothing is certain in this world. Connections and love are hard to come by. People with integrity, substance, and genuine natures are scarce. So if you can find a person with those qualities who you can see yourself falling for, I'd say go for it. But to find a connection with a person and be turned off because that person has a child? I'm sorry . . . but I don't understand. When you deal with a child, a life can be changed."

"The kid's?"

"No. Yours."

He was silent for a moment, as if processing what I had said.

"I guess I never thought about it like that." He smiled and stared at me. "You know what? I like talking to you. You have an interesting way of conveying things to me."

"I'm a regular girl, just speaking firmly on what I believe."

"What are you eating?"

"Leftovers. Barbecue chicken quesadillas."

"Huh? What the . . . ?"

I chuckled and pushed my Tupperware bowl toward him. "Get some."

He was hesitant, but after he took a small piece and chewed, he took an even bigger piece.

"This is good. Can I have some more?"

"Go ahead."

He broke off another piece in my dish. "You can cook. James once told me you could. Believe me when I say that I have never dated a girl who can cook. And if they claimed they could, they never wanted to. They always wanted to go out to eat."

"Well, it's something I enjoy doing. And this is Sierra's favorite dish. I hope one day I can open up a little spot and make all my signature dishes."

"You're ambitious too?"

"Without a doubt."

"You know, in going back to what you just said, you have a way of saying things and helping me see them in a different light. You are an enlightening person, Allure."

Funny, I never thought someone like him would find anything enlightening about me. Interesting. And I guess he wasn't all that bad.

I was relieved that day, when I was in my seventh period class. As the bell rang and students started trickling in, I took a few sips of water and grabbed my roll book. I was surprised when two girls and a boy I didn't recognize came and sat in my classroom. But this sometimes happened when they played around and tried to play hooky from another class.

I chuckled at them and said, "Okay. You three need to go to your correct class."

One of the girls got really angry and shouted, "Bitch, I'm in the right class!"

"You don't call Ms. Jones a bitch! Bitch!" Xavier, one of my students, shouted.

"Fuck up, nigga!" said the boy I didn't recognize.

"Stay out of it," I told Xavier before he could say anything else. I turned back to my three intruders. "You three have three seconds to leave my class, or I'm calling campus security."

I counted to three, and they didn't budge. I turned, about to walk to my phone. Before I could take a second step, I was ambushed. They all attacked me. They were punching and kicking the hell out of me.

The boy landed a punch so fierce, I fell to the floor, where I was assaulted some more. Xavier ran forward and shielded my body with his to stop me from getting attacked further. But the three intruders were relentless. I had no idea why they would want to attack me. I had never even seen these students before in my life.

"Someone get campus security!" I yelled.

One of my students exited the class. When the three intruders started attacking Xavier to get to me and assault me further, two of my female students rushed forward and started fighting with the two girls. That gave Xavier and another one of my male students, Dale, the opportunity to attack the boy who was attacking me. I attempted to break the four girls up, because I didn't want my students to get hurt. I grabbed one of my attackers by the back of her shirt and slammed her. When she attempted to get up off the floor, I held her down, and I commanded my two female students to hold down the other girl.

Thank God, Omar rushed into the classroom. He immediately attempted to separate the boys who were fighting. Seconds later, campus security came and assisted him. They were able to break up the fighting and restrain all three of my attackers.

As campus security escorted them out of my class, the boy turned, looked at me, and said, "That's for getting Angel arrested, you bitch!"

My eyes widened. The bitch had put them up to this. *Lord, have mercy,* I thought. *She just isn't going to stop her madness. First, she kidnaps my child. Now this.*

My lip was busted and the inside of my mouth was cut from the young man punching me. But that was it. The principal and I sat in his office so I could have some privacy. When one of the police officers finally came into the office, I explained what had happened and told him what the young man had said about Angel. I could not believe that this had just happened to me.

"You may or may not have to testify against them in juvenile court," the cop told me. "They will contact you if they need you to come down to the court."

"That is fine."

"The young man admitted that he is the cousin of Angel Trickman. And she ordered him to assault you," the cop added.

I closed my eyes briefly and shook my head.

"Well, this could possibly be another charge for her."

I nodded. "Thank you. Do you need anything else, Officer?"

"Nope. You're free to go."

"Are you sure you're okay?" my principal asked me.

"Yep. Just ready to go home."

"Have a good day, Allure."

"Thanks." I stood, left the office, and walked to my classroom.

Omar walked in my classroom. "Are you okay?" he asked me as I held an ice pack the school nurse had given me, to my mouth.

I smiled and nodded as I gathered my things.

"Who is Angel?"

I lied. "An old student I gave an F to." There was no way I was going to tell him the truth. And I hoped that James never mentioned anything about Greg or that crazy bitch.

"Damn, Allure. That was crazy. Your kids must care about you to jump in like they did."

I chuckled. "Yep."

A flashback of the boy punching me passed before my eyes. Made me think about the times that Greg had done the same to me. How brutal of that young man to even put his hands on a woman in that fashion. It was like Greg and the drama he brought was never ending. I was just glad I wasn't severely hurt from this mess. And I hoped they kept that bitch locked down for a while.

Chapter 10

It was time for my second official date with Chris. I counted our meeting at Kendra's house as the first one. He had decided to take me to Santa Monica Pier. In all honesty, I hadn't been there since James. I hated going back to places that I had been to with my ex, because it always brought me back to that place when I was in love and happy. And then to go back and have just memories sucked. But I willed myself to have a good time. We walked around, hand in hand, and enjoyed all the festivities. He asked me if I wanted to eat at Bubba Gump Shrimp Company, but I told him I was cool eating the pier food, so we snacked on corn dogs, funnel cake, chili cheese fries, and Slurpees. We did the bumper cars and video games, and played the music game *Guitar Hero*. We then competed against each other at the *Hoops* game and *Dance Dance Revolution*. I was having a good time.

We even went over to the ladder challenge, where people tried to climb a ladder to win a big stuffed teddy bear. The problem with it was that as you attempted to climb the ladder, it would spin, knocking you off. When I was with James, I used to beg him to play that game so he could win me a big bear. But instead of playing, he just went and bought the bear. It wasn't the same.

"Bet you won't try that," I challenged.

"Try what?"

I pointed to the ladder as a man attempted to climb up it. He kept losing his balance as it twisted.

"Aww, baby." He started stretching his arms and legs. "You just sit tight. I will be right back."

After he paid, I laughed as I watched him struggle up the rope ladder. As it spun around, he used his strong arms to grip it and he was able to hold on. A crowd formed around him as he successfully climbed up four steps. His fingers slipped on one step, but he did not fall off. His legs were still able to hold on. He took his time and went up three more steps on the ladder. He was breathing hard and sweating, but he still hung on.

"I better get a good kiss for this," he told me.

I laughed and watched him pull himself up the next three steps. When he got to the top step, he said, "Which one you want, baby?" There was a giant panda bear, a Superman, and a giant Tigger.

"Tigger!"

He snatched it and came down. The whole crowd laughed and cheered. When he walked toward me with the Tigger, he said, "I'm a fireman. What you expect, baby?"

I laughed again, grabbed his face in my hands, and gave him a peck on the lips. I was flattered that he was willing to embarrass himself for me, something James would never do.

Our final amusement was the Ferris wheel. Although I was scared to get on, I didn't tell him. I mean, what date at an amusement park was complete without the pair getting on the Ferris wheel? I knew how it went. So we got on, and Chris wrapped his arms around me.

As it went up, he asked me, "Are you having a good time?"

"Yep. Thank you."

"Anytime. I plan on keeping that pretty smile on your face."

I smiled at that. And then . . . Let's just say the unthinkable happened.

Cramps started hitting my stomach, each one stronger than the previous one, letting me know I needed to take a shit immediately.

I felt a fart coming on, so I squeezed my butt cheeks together and prayed to God it didn't come out. But as I squeezed my cheeks, I wiggled in the seat from the cramps.

"You okay?"

I nodded.

But another fart came, and I held my breath as I continued to squeeze my butt cheeks. More cramps hit me. I had two options: I could try to hold it, and pray it didn't come out, or I could get the fuck off the ride. But I didn't want Chris to know I had to take a serious poop. How damn romantic was that? *Why does shit like this have to happen to me?* I thought.

I could feel a turd trying to push its way out. It would be more embarrassing to poop on myself than to just try to get off the Ferris wheel.

"Stop the ride!" I yelled, clutching my stomach.

"Huh?" Chris looked at the ride attendant and flagged him, yelling, "Hey! Stop the ride. My lady friend is sick!"

The attendant mumbled something, shook his head, and brought the ride to a close. As soon as we were lowered and I was able to get out, I took off running. But before I could get into gear, I tripped on the Ferris wheel's long extension cord and fell to the ground.

"Allure!" Are you okay?" Chris lifted me by my forearms back onto my feet. I was hit with another cramp, and then I farted! Embarrassed, I took off running again to the nearest bathroom. Once I found it, I rushed past people and went into a stall, praying I didn't shit on myself before putting my ass on the seat.

There were no seat covers.

"Damn! Damn! Damn!" I made a seat cover out of tissue by tearing off several four-square strands and placing them on all sides of the toilet seat. Then I made a sigh of relief and sat down. Me letting it all out sounded like an explosion in the toilet. My stomach continued to lurch, and I continued to poop until I thought I would never poop again. At one point I thought I was finally done, so I slowly wiped my ass and pulled my pants back up, but then I felt the cramps come on again. So I pulled my pants back down, made another seat cover, and let it all out in the porcelain bowl. I tried a second time to wipe my ass and get up. But I had to go yet again. It was some serious diarrhea. I pulled out my phone and texted Creole.

On a great date at Santa Monica Pier with a great guy and guess where I am right now? On a shitter!

She texted me back.

LMAO! Only you, Allure Jones. Your asshole is playing tricks on you!

I texted, I was hoping you would make me feel better.

My name not Pepto-Bismol.

I didn't respond, because I was hit with more cramps and I was shitting heavily.

A set of flats appeared under my stall. There was a knock, and I heard the voice of an elderly lady. "Are you Allure?"

I moaned on the toilet. "Yes."

"A guy name Chris is outside the bathroom. He asked me to check on you and make sure you're okay."

Another explosion from my ass erupted into the toilet bowl.

"Tell him I'm fine and I'll be out in a second, please."

"Okay, honey."

I saw her heels walk away. And I could hear her say, "Oh, she's just pooping. She said she is fine."

Oh, God. Why did she have to tell him that?

It was some serious diarrhea. Thank goodness I had some Imodium A-D. Approximately fifteen minutes later, I popped two Imodium A-Ds and washed them down with some faucet water and exited the bathroom. Embarrassed out of my mind, I spotted Chris standing outside the restroom, waiting for me.

When I made it back over to him he handed me my Tigger, and kissed me on one of my cheeks. "Are you okay?" he asked me.

"Yep. I just think the food made me sick."

"Okay. Well, let me get you home so you can get some rest."

We walked back to the car in silence. It was weird and an awkward silence. I didn't know what the hell to say. I had probably grossed his ass out. *Towards the end of a great date, I get the shits! Only me!* I thought.

It was the same on the ride home. "Are you okay?" He asked me looking my way.

I nodded and stared out the window.

When we made it to my house he said he turned to me and said "I had a good night. Call me when you get settled in."

"Okay," I said, not looking his way. I was still too damn embarrassed. Instead I pulled off my seat belt and grabbed my purse. I heard his seat belt unsnap as well. Suddenly when I looked up I screamed. At the horrible vision in front of me.

"What baby?"

"Look!" I pointed at this big ass opossum chilling on my porch there were four baby opossums in tow.

I continued to scream as his gold eyes were on us in the truck.

"Aww babe that's just an opossum."

"Rats, opossum, gerbals, guina pigs, hamsters, ferrets, armadillo same damn thing!"

He chuckled. "Relax baby."

"Relax? You don't see that big ass rat?"

He chuckled. "They're fearful of humans. Watch this. I'll scare it away."

He honked his horn and the baby opossums scurried away in fear. But instead of the opossum running away the opossum hissed and that crazy motherfucker leaped on the windshield of the truck.

I yelled at the top of my lungs and closed my eyes.

"I got this baby. He got out the car and grabbed my push broom that rested against the wall of my house. He swiped at the possum until it fell from the truck.

Then he turned and walked towards me. "See baby. You safe now."

Next thing I knew the possum leaped onto Chris's right pants leg and crawled up his body. Chris struggled to get it off of him.

I screamed, jumped out the car fearfully and grabbed the push broom. I swing at the opossum hitting Chris in his back. "I'm sorry Chris!" I swung again and knocked the opossum down. He lay flat for a few seconds and the next thing I knew, the opossum was now back standing. He hissed and charged at me.

"Shit!" I screamed and started running for my life and that little fucker was on my heels.

"I got him baby!" I heard Chris yell.

I turned around and saw Chris's foot planted on the opossums tail so he couldn't move. He had a box in his hands.

He continued to hiss. "Baby. Go in the house and let me deal with this."

I was breathing hard and nodded." Okay." I continued to run towards the house. I dove into the car and got my purse and keys. I quickly unlocked my door and ran inside locking it back.

A few minutes later I heard my cell ring. It was Chris. "Did you kill it?" I demanded.

He chuckled. "Yes baby. I had to. "

"So what did you do with it?"

"I have it in my truck. I'm going to go dispose of it now. But just know you're safe. I'm a little pissed though."

"Why you wanted to keep it as a pet?"

"No. I didn't get my kiss."

"Oh." I blushed. "I'll make up for that on the next date." I was glad the opossum distracted Chris from my diarrhea.

"Good night."

"Bye." Once we both hung up I called Creole.

"What's up, shitty?" she said.

"Bitch!" I snapped

She cracked up laughing in my ear.

"It was the best night ever, and I had to get diarrhea."

"I know. Only you."

"But girl that's not the worst of it. There was a big ass bionic possum hanging out on my porch!"

"Aww shit. You sure that wasn't Greg?"

I busted up laughing.

"But how is he?"

"Really cool. Kendra said I would like him, and I do."
She chuckled.

"What? He must be cool. This is the first time you started a convo without mentioning James's punk ass."

"Do I mention him that much?"

"Well, you been in love with him for years, girl. I'm used to it. Someway, somehow, you would revert back to him. If this fireman can help you stop thinking about his punk ass, then I'm all for it, you know. And if he likes you, the fact that you had to take a shit on your date is not going to stop him from liking you or wanting to see you again."

"You think so?"

"Yes, you dummy."

I chuckled, relieved.

"So much fun. We got on the bumper cars, played some games, and he won me a Tigger!"

"Finally, a man won you that shit."

"Yep. And we got on the Ferris wheel. And that's when I had to use the bathroom—"

"Hold on! You were in the air and got the shits?" She busted up laughing again, to the point where I thought she was going to choke.

"Shut up!" I said.

My line clicked. It was Chris.

"Hold on, Creole!" I clicked over to Chris quickly. "Hello?"

"Hey, babe."

I smiled, and my heartbeat sped up. He was still interested.

"I just wanted to let you know that I really had a good time with you, Allure. And I can't wait for the opportunity to go out with you again."

"Awww. Thank you. I really had a good time as well."

"Okay. Well, drive safe. I'm glad Kendra introduced you to me. I get a head start on wining you over before another man does."

"You're making me blush."

"Get used to that. Like I said earlier, I plan on keeping that pretty smile on your face."

"I look forward to that."

"Good night."

"Bye." I ended the call and clicked back over to chop it up with Creole about my date.

Over the next three weeks Christopher and I went on a series of dates. We went to Skate Depot on couples' night. It was so cool to skate around and hold hands with a guy. I loved the feeling of that newness when you were getting to know someone and it was all good. The thing I liked about Christopher was the fact that he was such a Southern gentleman—the way James was in the very beginning. Every single date he took me on, he always came with some flowers. On our third date he took me to Benihanas. The fourth date was to San Antonio Winery, and the fifth was skating.

The only difficulty was making the time to see him. Thing was, Christopher wanted to spend more time with me than I had. Because I had a child, I couldn't just see him freely like he wanted and even like I wanted to. But that was the sacrifice you made when you dated a woman with a kid. He said that he was cool with it and that he simply had a genuine interest in getting to know me. Kendra said he was constantly gushing about me to Elijah. During that time James managed to tiptoe his way in. He came to more of Sierra's games, and he even managed to come over again for dinner.

One night I was on the phone, talking to Christopher, and cooking dinner when I heard the doorbell. James stood there like he was coming home to his wife. I ended my call quickly and stood in my doorway, looking at him like he was crazy.

"Hey, babe."

"Not your babe, James. What are you doing, popping up?"

"Sierra didn't tell you? She texted me and asked me to come over."

That was it. I had to talk to her little ass. I knew she loved James, but she couldn't just invite him over anytime she wanted to. She needed to ask me first.

"Sierra!" I called. Enough was enough. I had to get on her about doing things without telling me.

She ran into the room. "Yes, Mommy?"

"Why did you invite James over without telling me?"

Before she could respond, the home phone rang. She walked over to the computer desk and grabbed it and answered it. "Hello. Who's calling?"

James laughed. "She still answers the phone the same way, huh?"

I rolled my eyes at him. "If it's Chris, tell him I'll call him back."

James's eyes narrowed.

Suddenly Sierra gasped.

"Who is it?" I asked.

She closed her eyes briefly. "It's a collect call from Daddy. He's in jail."

For approximately sixty seconds I listened to Greg babble about getting involved in some bullshit. He had beaten up his new girlfriend because she was angered by the fact that he got tickets to the Soul Train Awards and didn't take her. He said he'd been sentenced to twenty-three months for domestic abuse. What the hell was I supposed to tell his ass? And when I tried to give the phone to Sierra, he asked me not to. He wanted to carry on a conversation with me. He even had the nerve to ask me in one breath to put money on his books and get him a calling card. And then in the next breath he blamed me for him being locked up, because if I had not left him six years before, he wouldn't be in this situation. So I ended the call. I sat the phone down, took a deep breath, and patiently explained the situation to Sierra, all while James sat there, looking angry.

I watched tears slide down Sierra's face.

"Come here, Sierra," James said.

She did, and James pulled her onto his lap and started hugging her. "It's okay, baby. Cry. Get it out." And she did. She sobbed on his lap.

I knew it wasn't just because Greg had been locked up. It was because of all the years of promises and letdowns, all the disappointments her father had brought to her. I knew, because over the years I had wiped many tear-stained, snot-nosed faces and given plenty of hugs. But it never took away the pain she felt. Only her father could, by being right, by being a real and loving father to her. And in all honesty, I knew he probably never would. This was the type of Dad he had chosen to be to her. And only he could change it. And if he was going to, I felt he would have done it by now.

A few minutes later, Sierra got up and went to her room. I waited a few minutes and then went to check on her. But she said that she didn't want to be bothered, that she didn't want to talk about it. So I left her alone and went back into the living room. I sat on the couch.

"Allure, when are you going to accept the fact that her daddy ain't shit and he is never going to be shit?"

"It's her daddy, James."

"He ain't no Daddy, Allure. He ain't shit. He is going to keep disappointing her."

I started crying out of frustration. "So what am I supposed to do?"

"Allure, baby, he doesn't want her. I want her. Let me by her godfather. I'll do for her all his sorry ass won't do."

"How are you going to do that when you have two kids and a wife?"

"I'll find a way. Let me know about all her games, and I'll be there. I will also spend one day a week with her. Maybe take her to the arcade or to a movie. I'm honestly not out to get shit out of this. I just want to be there for her. For all the wrong I done to you, I feel like I owe you this."

"What about your wife? How in the hell is she going to be okay with this?"

"Look, don't concern yourself with her. As long as I provide for my kids and I'm there in our bed every night, she should have nothing to say. As long as I am able to balance it all without neglecting anyone, that's all that should matter. Spending time with Sierra once a week is not going to affect my family."

What could I say to his suggestion? What he was saying about her father was the truth. And I knew there was a missing part in Sierra's life because her dad wasn't actively in it. I knew this because there was a missing piece in my heart that had been with me forever. Growing up, I would have given anything to have some type of father figure in my life. I didn't want Sierra making bad choices because she didn't have a father's love. I knew this was an easy thing to do, looking at myself and the choices I had made. And maybe this could work.

I gave James a serious look. "If we do this, there has to be some rules involved."

He nodded eagerly, making me once again second-guess whether this arrangement was for Sierra or for me. But I guess it really didn't matter as long as he was willing to follow my rules.·

"I don't want you popping up, period. For any reason at all. And don't call or text me. Sierra has a cell. So there really is no need for you to contact me. And when you come to visit her, please do not be trying to hang around me. I'm not sleeping with you."

"I got it, Allure."

"I'm not done."

For the next twenty minutes I explained to Sierra that James was going to be back in her life. She seemed bothered by the fact that her daddy had been locked up, but upon learning that James was going to be coming around more, she brightened up. While I finished up dinner, he helped her out with her homework and then they battled each other on *Just Dance.* When my dinner of barbecue ribs, mac and cheese, string beans, and corn bread was done, James sat down with us to eat. It felt too much like old times. But then, at the same time, I appreciated James for agreeing to do this. If he let my daughter down with broken promises and lies, I was going to have his ass.

After dinner I talked to Chris on the phone. When he asked how my day was, I told him. "A mess."

"Why, baby?"

I was smart enough not to mention what had happened with Greg. I was wise enough to know not to bring up my past with a man. Hell, no. They would take that shit and run with it. And although I had a lot of love for James, I liked Chris. Seemed like everything in my life was coming together. With the situation with Greg and James being resolved, I was able to sleep peacefully.

The next day, during my third period class, I spent my time discussing what a soliloquy was and showing how crybaby Richard from Shakespeare's *Richard III* delivered them throughout the whole play. At one point, a delivery guy came into my room with a fruit bouquet from Edible Arrangements.

"Miss Jones is a pimp," Josh, one of my students, said. I chuckled.

"Who is it from, Miss Jones?" Candy, another student, asked while smacking gum.

I smiled and read the card. It was from Chris. I blushed. The card read, *Can't wait to see you tonight.*

The other night he had said he was having a dinner party and he was having some guests over and he wanted me to come. I was going to have to hurry once my day at work was done. I had to run home, shower, get dressed, go to Sierra's game, and then go to Chris's house from there.

"It is probably from Mr. Collins. That fool stay trying to hit Miss Jones up." That was Josh again.

The class exploded in laughter, and I heard a few of my students agree.

Another said, "Yeah. His ass. Do. Always up in here."

I looked at the pretty bouquet, which had pineapples and strawberries dipped in milk and white chocolate.

"Settle down, you guys, and let's get focused again." The laughter and the whispers stopped, and they regained their focus. One thing I was always serious about was class time. I was no-nonsense.

During lunch that day, Omar stopped by my class.

"Hey," he said. He had two Styrofoam containers in his hands.

"What's up?"

He looked around. "For the first time, your class is actually empty. Is it because of the report cards?"

Report cards were due on Monday. "Nope. I turned mine in already. You?"

"I am nowhere near done. They are stressing the hell out of me. But I will get them done by Monday. So where exactly are you going?"

I grabbed my purse. "It's because I have a doctor's appointment. I'll be back, though."

He looked disappointed. "Probably when class is back in session. I picked up some Thai food last night, and I was thinking about you and I brought you some."

"Awww. That was sweet of you. But I can't sit and eat with you. But thanks."

"You are very welcome." He handed me one of the containers.

"Thanks. I owe you."

"I'm going to hold you to that, Allure."

I smiled, a little nervous, and walked out of the classroom. I could have sworn he was flirting with me.

My checkup took a little longer than usual because my doctor said that when she examined my breasts and squeezed, there was a discharge coming from my nipples. She said it was normal to have a discharge, but she wanted to give me a complete exam. She did what was called a ductogram. That shit hurt. She inserted a thin plastic tube into the opening of my nipple and injected me with some shit, and then my breast was x-rayed. Once that was done, I was just happy the shit was over, and I could get back to work and then get my ass home and start my weekend.

When I got back to class, I breezed through the rest of the day. And since it was Friday, my kids wasted no time running out of class when the school bell rang. Just as I grabbed my things to walk out of my class, Omar stepped through the door.

"I just came back to tell you to have a good weekend."

I chuckled. "Well, thank you, Omar."

"So what are your plans?"

He walked up to me and stood with his arms crossed over his chest.

"Well, I'm going to my daughter's game, and then I'm going to a dinner party with some friends."

"Do you need a date?"

I gave him a weird look.

"You look so pretty today."

Before I could stop him, he leaned in and kissed me.

I pulled back. "Omar!" I pushed him away and wiped my lips.

"I'm sorry. I have been wanting to do that for a long time. I mean, I wanted to know how your lips tasted. Allure, you have some pretty, soft, kissable lips."

"Look, Omar. Forget what you thinking, because it is not going to go down. Not now and not ever. In fact, you need to leave my classroom."

"I'm sorry. I didn't mean to upset you." But he still stood there.

"Please leave my room."

He nodded, turned, and walked out of my classroom.

Shaken up by what he had just done, I took a couple deep breaths and left.

Chapter 11

The kiss had me a little shaken up. It was not something I was expecting at all. I asked myself silently if I had given him the impression that I liked him, and the answer was no. I didn't know what was in that arrogant mind of his that had made him think that I wanted that. All I was trying to do was get along with his ass, keep the peace for the sake of my job, and he clearly misunderstood my intentions. I wiped the incident out of my mind and rushed home.

Once I got there, I showered, shaved, applied lotion on my entire body, and got dressed. I wore a pretty pink and gray dress that cinched at the waist with a belt and billowed out at the bottom, on my thighs. I wore some gray suede heels to bring out the pretty gray in the dress. For tonight I did the works: I put on foundation, eye shadow, lined my lips, and wore some plum lipstick. I was looking good. I grabbed my purse and coat and rushed out so I could make it to the game. When I got there, I was just a few minutes late. I saw James, and surprisingly, Creole was sitting next to him. She had agreed to take Sierra with her once the game was over.

"Oh, shit, hooker," she joked, eyeing my outfit with approval.

And James, he wouldn't stop looking at me. It was like I was the basketball game. I sat down on the other side of Creole, nodding at James and chuckling. He nodded back, looked at me one more time, and turned his focus back to Sierra. Creole and I both scooted over some so we could talk.

"Wow. Since when are you cool with James?" I whispered in her ear.

"Since he knocked the fuck out of your baby daddy. After all the horrible things he did to you, Greg deserved that. And you know what? James and I got here a little early, and we talked. He told me about this little arrangement you seemed to forget to mention to your child's godmother."

"I didn't want you to judge me. Or to think I'm messing around with him again."

"Allure, if you were to take James and fuck him on chocolate-covered grass, I wouldn't judge you, so get that out of your head. I actually think it's a good idea."

I looked at her, surprised.

"He did some fucked-up stuff, no doubt. But one thing I know about the nigga is he always cared about you and Sierra. And as long as he keeps his word, it's cool. And two, from the sound of this dude, Christopher seems like he is a decent guy as well. We don't know for sure, because it's still too soon to tell, but I think you should keep doing what you doing all around. Sierra seems happy, and you do too."

I smiled. I was. I wanted to tell her about Omar kissing me at work and ask her what the best thing to do about it was, but when I looked up at James, I saw that he was trying his hardest to ear hustle, so I made a mental note to tell her later.

"So how is the walking scum of the earth?"

"Girl bye with that."

"But he talked so much shit in court that day about you being a horrible mother and him being such an outstanding father, blah fucking blah. Meanwhile, you had your baby bit up so bad she looked like one of those kids in Ethiopia, so you could get some from your dirty rat girlfriend."

"Right." I thought back to the time after Sierra had accumulated all the mosquitos bites and I wouldn't let him see her anymore. *One day I came home and was more down shocked to find out that Greg had filed papers on me with the courts.*

He was fighting me for joint custody of Sierra. His orders were ridiculous. Greg wanted to keep Sierra Monday, through Friday and overnight Wednesdays and Thursdays. He also put that I needed to get his permission before leaving Sierra with anyone else other than him. I almost cracked up as I sat on the couch after a long day of work and read his statement. It read.

I am requesting joint custody of my child Sierra Richman. Her mother, Allure Jones has gone out of her way to prevent me from forming a strong relationship with my daughter. She will not let me see her and refuses my phone calls. I have been active in my daughter's life since she was born and have been supporting my child since she was born although the money never goes to my child. Allure Jones is angry that I have moved on and no longer have a desire to be with her. She is using my daughter as a tool to hurt me. I am also asking that Allure Jones be made to take parenting classes. I think she would benefit from this I also think Allure Jones is a bad role model for my daughter and her lifestyle choices are very questionable. I am also requesting child support to properly care for my daughter. Oh and Allure does drugs. I live with my soon to be wife and I would like my daughter to live with me as well.

I wanted to scream. I threw the papers in disgust. After all he has subjected me to and after all he has not done for my daughter he had the never to not only lie but to try to take me to court. I swear Greg had reached an all-time new low. I wondered if this "soon to be wife is the same home he took Sierra to when she got bit up. There was no way he should be alone with Sierra again. I prayed the judge didn't give him what he was asking for.

The day we went to court I sat in the court room and tried to remain calm. I wouldn't even look Greg's way while we waited outside for them to open the doors.

Even as the doors opened and he stood next to me he had the nerve to say, "Hi Allure."

But my vision was tunnel and all I was concerned with was getting this shit over.

When it was our turn and we were called to the table to sit in front of the judge

The judge a new one named Clay reviewed the paperwork and said, Okay what is your position on this case Mr. Richman?"

"Plain and simple Allure Jones is an unfit mother. She doesn't take good care of my daughter. She is so torn with her anger and jealously that it prevents her from ummm . . . Co-parenting with me. I don't' want her I've moved on with my life. I have a good woman, we now live together and she just can't accept that it is over between us. I didn't have my father growing up, so I want to be in Sierra's life. I believe my soon to be wife and I can properly raise Sierra. I'm doing this for my child. So ummm. That's where I stand."

"What is your response to this Ms. Jones?"

"In my response to the petition, there are also police reports and a letter from my doctor showing what type of father Greg has been. What Greg is saying are all lies. I love my child to a degree that a man like him could not even begin to understand. Because of this I would never intentionally hurt my child by keeping her from her father. The problem is he has never been a father. Maybe had things not been about me than maybe Greg would have been somewhat of a father. I didn't come here to drag his name in the mud. But what you can do is run his

record and see that he has a history of domestic violence against women. He has recently neglected my daughter. He did not follow the court order and in doing so he took my daughter and had her over someone's house and she was bit up so bad by fleas that her doctor said they will leave permanent scars. I admit I stopped letting him see her because I'd rather have him out of her life and safe than him in it and unsafe. I work. I don't have a record, Sierra is well loved and cared for. I also don't do drugs. You can test me now if you like. If you want to permanently test me feel free. I'm not who Greg is trying to paint me to be. But he knows. He knows me well. I would like for Greg to do monitored visitation again."

"I can't afford that!" he yelled. "I'm a black man trying to make it in this racist ass world and you the black bitch trying to keep me down!.."

"No outbursts." The bailiff said.

"What do you do?" the judge asked me.

"I'm a high school English Teacher."

"What do you do?" he asked Greg.

"I'm a security guard."

"The agreement before was for the child to be seen at your mother's house. Mr. Richman. You need to follow the order because I am not changing it. In fact, I doubt that I ever will," he said sternly. "You are not allowed to take the child out of the grandmother's care. You may visit her at your mother's house and that's it. Matter of fact, if you ever do so again. Allure will have the power to call the Police and have you arrested."

"What do you mean to tell me that you not going to take my daughter away from that-"

I stared straight ahead.

"She will continue to have sole and legal custody. If you take the child anywhere, I don't care if it's to the store or up the street, you will be arrested and I will have *your parental rights revoked. You have been getting off easy. Not anymore."*

"But this is the order we've had," I interjected. "He didn't follow it."

"Well he is standing on his last leg and this time if he doesn't follow the order he will face criminal charges. It shows that you are still on probation so I'll add probation condition #TwentyTwo. You are not allowed to go to any public place with a child and if you do you will be arrested and your parental rights as I said, will be revoked."

Okay for the first time that day I caught a glimpse of Greg, His eyes were wide and he looked shook when the judge spoke on probation.

"One more thing Judge. He does not pay child support. Your honor I asked him to give me one hundred dollars a month and he refused."

The entire courtroom burst in laughter.

"How much do you make?" the judge asked Greg.

"I just got hired so I-ah. I don't know."

"How much hourly?"

"I make sixty dollars every two weeks."

More laughter in the courtroom.

Even the lady typing was giggling.

"Okay. I gonna put in an order for you to receive two hundred dollars a month."

"What!" that's when things got crazy.

"I take care of my child!" he yelled.

"His definition of taking care of Sierra is every Christmas bringing her some toys from the ninety nine cents store. Around the clock, winter, spring, summer fall I am providing all the needs she has and it has been this way all these years."

"Okay well we'll put in the order. We are done here."

"No were not done!" Greg yelled. "Matter fact, why am I here?"

"Because you filed paper," the judge said evenly.

Well I'm not done. I-_ "

Before he could say another word he was escorted out of the courtroom by the bailiff.

I would have preferred the monitored visitation but since this was all I could get and it was better than Greg getting my child I left it alone. And it was only twice a month. So I was okay with it. Not really . . . But I accepted it. I left the courtroom and Greg and I ended up on the same elevator. I pretended he wasn't there and refused to look his way even once.

"Get it Sierra!" Creole yelled snapping me out of my thoughts.

"The good thing is that Sierra is not worse for wear you know? Despite what he has and hasn't done as a father she is just fine."

"I know," I said. "I just wish things were different."

After the game, I gave Sierra a hug and twenty bucks, as Creole was taking her to a movie, and they went off, leaving me with James.

"Let me walk you to your car," he said.

I didn't protest, because I knew if I did, he would walk me, anyway. As we walked, I debated whether to tell him about what his brother had done. I decided to leave it alone. I didn't want to get into a big discussion when I had somewhere to be.

"You look nice, Allure. Those colors look really pretty on you. I don't remember you ever wearing much pink when we were together."

"I was in denial. Too embarrassed to admit that this girly color was my favorite."

He chuckled.

When we made it to my car, I was hoping he walked his ass on away, but of course he didn't.

"You going somewhere special tonight?"

"A friend's dinner party."

"Who?" he asked bluntly.

"James, you know that's none of your business," I said firmly.

"I know. . . . It's just that I . . ." His eyes traveled up and down my body.

I softened my voice. "Just let me go, okay?"

He looked away and nodded. "Bye."

I waved, then turned to get in my car. He stood there, watching me, even after I started up the car and backed out and drove forward. I could still see him standing there when I exited the parking lot. It was killing him to know about my love life.

I stood nervously on Christopher's porch steps. I knocked, then clapsed my hands together. I guess I was scared that I wouldn't fit in with his friends or that they plain out wouldn't like me. I had never been a social butterfly. My sister was. I had never quite fit in anywhere I had gone in my life. For some reason, I always managed to stand out, even when I didn't want to.

When the door opened and Chris appeared, I took him in. He looked so handsome in a light blue polo shirt, a pair of jeans, and a pair of Kenneth Cole loafers. I knew that was what they were because James had owned a pair.

"Hey, baby," he said. I blushed when he stepped close to me and hugged me. He smelled so yummy. He then kissed me on my right cheek. Then he stepped back and said, "Let me look at you." He twirled me until I was back facing him. "You look so pretty."

"Thank you."

He kissed me again—this time on my lips. I didn't object. I enjoyed the peck. Then, before I could shy away, he grabbed one of my hands and pulled me into his house.

When we stepped inside, he didn't let my hand go as he introduced me to his friends. There were three very handsome men at a table, playing cards, while three women lounged on both of his couches.

"These are the closest people to me," he said.

I thought it was cool that he hung out only with men who were in relationships.

Chris pointed as he introduced everyone. "This is West, and that's his fiancée, Dominic. Katrina is my cousin, and her man is Trey. And that big head is Clyde, and that's his lady, Ericka."

"Hello," I said.

They all smiled and said hello back.

"And you all have heard about her. Now you get to meet her. This is Allure," Christopher told them.

"Yes, we have," Dominic said sweetly. She was a very pretty, petite, dark-skinned lady.

"Come and sit down," Katrina said. I sat down next to her. She was chunky and had hazel-colored eyes and a short haircut. "I love your dress."

"Thank you."

"Babe, you want a drink?" Chris asked.

"Okay."

"A strawberry daiquiri?"

"Yes."

He walked off, and Ericka left the couch she was sitting on to sit next to me. She was friendly as well. She was my size and had my complexion. She had Chinese bangs, and the rest of her hair hung silkily around her shoulders.

"So we finally meet the oh-so-special Allure." Ericka winked at me.

I laughed. "I don't know about all that."

"Oh, but we do," Katrina chimed in. "He really likes you. . . . You don't catch the way he looks at you? He is my cousin, so I know him very well. There is a twinkle in his eye whenever he looks at you. He lights up like a Christmas tree."

I really didn't know what she was talking about. Then Chris came back with my drink.

I sipped on it and listened to their conversation. Katrina and Trey were married. Chris had actually introduced them to each other. Dominic was engaged to West, and Ericka said that Clyde was on the verge of proposing. So needless to say, Dominic talked my ear off about her upcoming wedding. And every time I looked up, I saw Chris looking my way.

"You don't see that twinkle, girl?" Katrina asked.

"I guess."

"Aww, don't be so modest, Miss Allure. Chris is a good man. If he has taken a liking to you, you must be special. Besides the fact that you are so naturally freaking pretty."

"Thank you."

I had never felt pretty. Growing up, I never had nice clothes and my hair always looked tacky, because we were poor. And after years of being hurt by men, I didn't feel attractive. Not at all. It felt good when these three beautiful black women told me that I was pretty.

Ericka asked the men, "Are you guys ready to eat?"

They all chorused, "Yeah."

I followed after the three ladies as they headed into the kitchen, and as I went, I caught Chris staring at me again. All three of the ladies grabbed plates. They started piling the plates high with stuffed pasta shells that were covered in a white cheese sauce, salad, and warm rolls.

As I grabbed a plate to fix one for Chris, I felt an arm slip around my waist. "You okay?" was whispered in my ear. I felt my heart pitter-patter. It was him. And having him that close to me felt really good, and so did his checking up on me. I liked it.

"I'm okay. I'm just making your plate."

"Chris, will you get out of here and let your woman make your plate?" Ericka said.

"Oh, I'm not his woman," I interjected quickly. But I wished I hadn't, because Chris seemed like he had liked how "your woman" sounded. His smile dropped after I uttered those words.

He winked at me and walked out of the kitchen.

Like the other women did with their men, I handed Chris his food. By this time the Lakers game was on, and the men were engrossed in the game. Katrina, Dominic, Ericka, and I went back into the kitchen and then made our own plates. We then took them outside on the deck to eat and talk.

The food was really good and flavorful. The shells were filled with tender chicken and shrimp. They asked me a million questions as we ate. They wanted to know everything about me. I even showed them pictures of Sierra on my cell phone. None of them had kids. I found out that Katrina was a registered nurse. Ericka worked at a preschool, and Dominic was a hairstylist. In a lot of ways she reminded me of my sister. I was sure that if they met, they would have a lot in common. The thought of my sister made me sad. I felt a little empty inside, but I tried to wipe out the sad thoughts and enjoy the night.

Stuffed, I sat my plate down on the table.

"I hope we didn't badger you too much, Allure. But since you're his women and all . . ."

Before I could reply, someone whispered in my ear, "Not yet, baby. Just say that."

I smiled as Chris kissed me on my cheek.

"Chris, you supposed to be with the men, not stalking Allure," Katrina joked.

"I want to spend some time with Allure."

Ericka laughed. "Maybe we should leave them alone."

All the ladies rose and grabbed their plates and glasses. They walked back into the house.

"Come over here, baby," Chris said after sitting down on a lawn chair.

I rose and walked over to him. I sat on the lawn chair beside him, happy to be near him. That man seriously gave me butterflies. He could be lying, but he seemed to like me just as much as I liked him. And he was a good man. *Man, please let this shit finally be true.*

"So how are you feeling?" he asked.

"Good. Everyone is so nice. I'm really having a good time."

"Good. I'm glad you enjoying yourself." He bit his bottom lip, still staring at me. Before I could stop him, he grabbed me by my forearms and pulled me into his lap. "I do bite, but come here, anyhow."

"Yeah, but will that bite hurt?" Damn. Why did I say that? I thought. *Damn, Allure. Shut up!*

"You know, not all men are out here ɔ hurt you, baby. There are some good men left, believe it or not." One of his arms wrapped around my waist, while his free hand played in my braids. "You know what? You look so pretty. You really are a beautiful woman. Inside and out."

"How you know?"

"'Cause, for one, I got eyes."

"I meant inside."

"I have the gift of discernment. And this past month I have been around you, it seems to me that everything about you is all things good and all things pure."

"I have never had a man tell me that before."

"Well, get used to it. You should be told nice things on a daily basis. You deserve to feel good. You deserve to feel happy. And—"

Before he could finish, I kissed him. A deep kiss involving his and my tongue, some serious tongue action. His arms tightened around me. This kiss was super passionate. When I pulled away, he groaned.

"And what?" I asked.

"I want to be the one from this point forward to keep a smile on your face."

Okay, I thought. Here was my dilemma. He was so fine and so, so sweet. He sounded sincere. But in the beginning they always sounded this way. I thought of Greg, Lavante, James, Bryce, and Andre. *Do I keep my guard up because of them, or do I let that shit go and enjoy this man? Just enjoy the moment? Or can I do both?* I willed myself not to make a decision. For the moment I was just going to enjoy myself. I deserved this.

I went back to making out with him. I had so much fun. After our make-out session, we went back inside and did karaoke and the Wobble. Not only was it a fun night, but I also think it brought me closer to Chris. I left his house with a big ole Kool-Aid smile on my face.

The next morning I got up, called Creole, and asked her when she was bringing Sierra home. She said she was putting some corn rolls in Sierra's hair, then they were going to go to a late breakfast, and then she would drop her off. So I started cleaning the house and doing our laundry. I threw some colored clothes in the washer. Then I set out to get the bathroom cleaned. I wanted to get all my cleaning done within an hour so I could do some grading.

As I cleaned the bathroom, I couldn't stop thinking about Christopher. He was so sweet to me. And all his friends had made me feel so comfortable. Chris was respectful and never gave me the impression he was trying to get in my pants. I could be wrong about him, because I had been wrong about men before, but I prayed I was right. After all the crap I had been through, I couldn't see myself being subjected to more. Plus, Kendra approved him. *So please, please, don't let him be a secret dog,* I thought. I had had enough of them to start a kennel. As I crouched down to scrub my toilet bowl, I heard my cell phone ring. I grabbed it out of my pocket and answered, not recognizing the number.

"Hello?"

"Hi, Allure. This is Omar."

"Hey, Omar? How did you get my number?"

I was actually glad he had called me. It would give me the opportunity to discuss what had happened the day before, when he had kissed me, and maybe it was better if we discussed it away from school.

"James, hey, I was wondering if you could do me a big favor. I'm not coming in on Monday, and I wanted to know if you could drop off my report cards with the sub for my class."

"That's fine. But you need to hurry, because I have things to do." *And I can also check you to your face.*

I gave him my new address, and he got to my house in twenty minutes. I did not hesitate to give him my new address. After all, he been to my home several times when James and I were together.

When I heard my doorbell ring, I mopped the rest of the bathroom floor quickly and laid the mop down.

"Hi, Omar," I said politely when I answered the door.

He smiled. "Hey, Allure."

I stepped aside to let him enter. We both sat down on my couch. He laid a large manila envelope on my coffee table.

"You know I have been feeling some kinda way since Friday," I told him.

He smiled. "Okay."

"What you did was out of line, for so many reasons. The first is the fact that it happened at work. I take my job very seriously, and stuff like that can't happen. Ever. Period." I let my eyes lock with his so he could see how serious I was. "And secondly, you know damn well I used to be involved with your brother. So I really don't know what you were thinking. You know I was with James and we had a child together. I'm still debating whether or not to tell him."

"Please don't. He already grills me on you as it is, like you two are still together. He wants to know if men come to see you and whatnot. Once I commented that you had nice cakes, and he acted like he wanted to beat my ass."

I shook my head at him. "See? You're playing with me. What you did was not cool and— "

"Okay. Well, first off, let me be a man and apologize for making you feel really uncomfortable at work. I don't know. I . . . The bottom line is that it was wrong. But a couple of months ago I started liking you. I enjoy your conversation, your spirit, the way you carry yourself. The way you are. How you care about the kids. You enlighten me. Usually, in a relationship I enlighten them. Thing is, James and his wife, when I'm around them, it is much different than the interaction between *you* and James. I always wondered why he did you the way he did you and didn't try to make it work."

"Really? You wondered this? Even when you treated me like shit on your doorstep?" I couldn't resist throwing it back in his face.

"I know. Back then I had disdain for single mothers. You changed my perspective on that by simply being who you are. So I say all this to say, you're special. And I want to see you. I don't care that you were once with my brother. It is his loss. And he fucked up. And I don't care that you have a child. I will love and accept Sierra like she is my own. Real talk."

I gasped at the craziness that was coming from this man's mouth.

"Are you insane?"

"No. I—"

"Listen to me carefully." I spoke slowly. "It can't happen. It won't happen. You are going to have to get it out of your head. I won't tell James, but you have to let your crush on me go. And remember we have to work together."

"Come on, Allure. I will treat you good. Let me show you."

"No."

He suddenly stood to his feet, like he was going to walk out. He paused and said, "Why won't you give me a chance?"

"You're James's brother. That is why."

"Why do you care about how he feels? He dogged you out. Treated you like shit. Why the fuck do you care what he thinks?"

I stood to my feet. "It's time for you to go." I attempted to walk toward the door, but he grabbed one of my arms and pulled me toward him.

"Why are you rejecting me? What you think? That you're better than me?"

"Get out of my house." I tried to pull away. He tightened his hold. He wrapped his arms around me so our bodies were touching and my arms were crushed by his body. He started kissing me. I tried to fight him off by struggling against him, because I couldn't use my arms. I managed to pull away from his lips. "Stop!"

I was about to scream when he crushed my mouth with his again. He backed me up toward the couch and lowered MC all while keeping his body over mine. A feeling of alarm hit me. He was going to rape me! I tried my best to fight him off, but he was far too big and far too strong. He straddled my body, all while still kissing me. He held both my hands in one of his and used his free hand to pull down my sweatpants. Tears were pouring from my eyes. I sobbed because I felt powerless to stop him from doing what he was doing. Still, I tried to fight.

When he moved his mouth away from mine, I screamed. He used his free hand to cover my mouth, and he tried to pull my panties down with his other hand. Then I didn't have to fight anymore, because my living room door burst open and James came running in. He took one look at us, and his eyes widened. Omar turned around and looked.

I moved away from his hands and yelled, "James, he is trying to rape me!"

For a second James looked torn. Then a look of rage took over his face. Before Omar could move, James grabbed him by the collar of his shirt and threw him off of me. He fell to the floor with a loud thud.

"Get up, motherfucker," James ordered.

His brother did, and James rushed him. And they were all out fighting in my living room.

As they threw punches, Omar said, "I would have treated her better than you, mothafucka."

That pissed James off more. He grabbed Omar and slammed him into the wall. Then they both went back to punching each other. James was beating his brother like he was going to kill him.

"James, that's enough! Stop!" I tried to grab one of James's arms and pull him off of his brother. He yanked away from me, causing me to fall backward. I stood back up and ran up to James and slapped him. "James! Stop it before you get arrested!"

He managed to snap out of it and shoved his brother away.

Chapter 12

After laying that ass whipping on his brother, James told me that however I wanted to handle the situation I could and he would support it. For me, that was calling the police and having Omar taken out in handcuffs. I had learned long ago not to let a man get away with trying to be physical in any way with me. As far as I was concerned, it would empower them, give them an inflated ego, and they would continue doing stuff like that. But I felt bad that James's brother was going to jail.

"You okay?" James asked me after the police had left.

I nodded.

"I can't believe he came over here and did that. I knew he could be aggressive. But . . ." He shook his head. "I never knew he would go this far. And especially with you." He pierced me with a glare. "What was he doing here?"

"James, don't even go on with your possessiveness when you have a wife. Don't you get that we haven't been together in over three years? You really don't have the right to question me in that manner. Now, if you are asking because he is your brother, then that's different."

"I'm sorry. Yes, I am jealous as hell. And if I said it is just because he is my brother—"

"You'd be a damn liar," I interrupted. "But you have to understand you don't have that right anymore, after all you have done."

"I know, but, baby, I still love you, so any man—my brother or a stranger—is going to make me hella jealous."

I looked away.

"But I will try to be more respectful and in control of my feelings. Now, what happened with my brother?"

I explained what had happened at work. And how Omar had asked if it was okay to drop off his report cards with me.

James looked furious when I mentioned that he had kissed me. "Why didn't you tell me he had kissed you?"

"I was going to. I just hadn't gotten around to it. It was no secret, because I have no interest at all in your brother. The last thing I needed or wanted was a problem like this. Did you give him my number?"

"No, he is obviously the one that caused the problem, not you, baby."

"I hoped I could resolve it by talking to him, and then it would be over. I hoped if we discussed it face-to-face, we could resolve it and come to an understanding. Squash it for the sake of us being able to work together." I felt so dumb for giving Omar my address. But who in the world would have thought he would pull some shit like that? Or react the way he reacted to my rejection? It gave me flashbacks of when Bryce had come over and attacked me because of the rumor that I was a man. It was like I had FUCK WITH ME tattooed on my forehead.

James shook his head, looking so heated.

There was something very important I wanted James to tell me. "But what about you? How did you just so happen to pop up here, James?"

"I know that I'm supposed to call before I come. But there are times where you are on my mind, and I find any excuse to head out this way. I'll say it's because I'm craving some tacos from the spot you put me on, on Pine Street. Just to have an excuse to drive down your street and hope I get a peek of you coming out to dump your trash or going to your car. And with you being a single woman with a child, I sometimes just want to make sure you are okay. Initially, it started with me just driving by from time to time these past three years. Then it's like the reemergence of feelings got stronger and stronger every day, to where I had to see you. So I would drive by more often, wanting to call you or even come to your doorstep. But for a long time I resisted the urge.

"Then, when your sister died, I had to be there for you. And after we made love, this shit got worse and worse. Like a fucking love jones, where I think about you day and night. I see your pretty face, Allure. I have fucking dreams where I'm fucking you and not my wife. I do wonder if you are with someone else, and if you will marry. It bothers me like hell.

"But today, as I drove by, I saw my brother's car in your driveway. He is the only person I know with SWERVE on his license plate. And a couple times I didn't mention that he told me he thought you were pretty and sexy. I thought he was doing it to make me jealous, because I shared with him that I still had strong feelings for you. But one night we were drunk, and he confessed that he liked you. But again, I never thought it would go this far. Nonetheless, I'm sure you are not happy about me driving by."

"That's the kind of stuff you just can't do if you want this arrangement to work."

"I know, and I'm sorry. I'll stop it. But I'm being honest with you. I'm not on some stalker shit. I just really care for you and Sierra."

"It's been three years, James. I wish you had cared more in the beginning and had made different decisions, but you didn't. I don't want to talk about any of it anymore. And I'm fine now, so you can go."

We both stood, and James followed me to the door. Once there he gave me a hug. I allowed it for a few seconds, before pulling away from him to watch him exit my house

It was another crazy day to add to my repertoire Just then my cell phone started ringing. It was James.

"Hello?"

"Can I ask you a question?"

"What?"

"I know it's none of my business, but are you seeing another man?"

"James . . ."

"Just answer please," he said, pressing.

"Not that it's your business, but yes."

He paused before asking, "It is serious?"

"No. But that doesn't mean that it won't be."

"Last question. If I wasn't married, would you give me another chance?"

Why did he want to hear this? It was not like he could reverse things at this point. I loved James still and had never wanted not to be with him. He was the only man I had loved these past three years, although we weren't together. For such a long time I couldn't see past him. Back then I didn't think I could be happy again without him in my life. My future no longer looked prosperous. In those days it looked bleaker, despite what I had accomplished: graduating college, getting a good job, buying my first home. I never felt complete, never experienced the amount of happiness I supposed I would feel if he were right there next to me to share in my accomplishments. Back then I experienced a lot of sick days, where I was running back and forth to the bathroom and had no desire to get out of my bed. I held on to a ridiculous hope that James's marriage was a hoax and he would come back to Sierra and me, but he never did.

When I gave up hope that he was coming back, I began to heal. So now, at this point, I did not want to revisit the pain that he had caused us. So I refused to entertain his notions about me now. For all I knew, he and his wife could be having problems and he was running to me for solace. Maybe he was just playing with me again. I refused to allow myself any hope that could lead me down that dark path he had led me down three years ago. But if he was serious, it made me feel bad for his wife and his kids. His kids didn't deserve to feel how I and Sierra had felt. And as much as I didn't like his wife for sleeping with my man, she didn't deserve the pain, either.

"Yes. But you are, so no need at all to wonder what this or that is . . . Good night." I ended the call.

Omar wasn't the only shocking guest to pay me a visit. The next day, when I was on my way to my car in the school parking lot, a gray Lexus pulled into the spot next to my car. A woman got out and walked over to me. After a few seconds I recognized her. She was James's wife. Although it had been three years since I'd last seen her, I believed that her face would always be imprinted on my brain. I thought back to the day I caught James in his truck with her, going down on her, while I was hidden behind the seats in back, big and pregnant. Then he turned around and married her ass.

"Before you ask, know that I do not want to fight with you. In fact, I want no trouble with you at all," she announced.

"Lady, you are showing up at my job."

"But I have never been near your home, and I know where it is as well. And I know how this looks I'm really sorry. But I desperately need to speak with you, if only for five minutes."

"You the same chick I caught fucking with James when I was pregnant. You didn't want to talk to me then, so you shouldn't want to talk to me now."

"We have something to talk about."

"We ain't got shit to talk about."

Her eyes got watery. "We have something to talk about. My husband. If we don't talk today, I will keep coming by until we do. I swear, just give me five minutes of your time and I will go away. Allure, please."

I rolled my eyes. "Five minutes. There is a park down the street. After five minutes if you're not done talking, I really won't care and I will leave you there. Real talk."

"Great. I'll follow you."

James had managed to get me caught up in his bullshit, when he had assured me it wouldn't be like this. I got in my car, shaking my head the whole time, and drove to the destination where I promised I'd meet her.

Once at the park, I walked over to a picnic table and sat down on one of the benches.

She followed and sat across from me. For a minute we just stared each other down. I had so much hatred for this woman. She had fucked my man, the love of my life, while I was pregnant. With no shame at all. And I had lost him to her, the supposed *better* woman. I had never seen her as better. Not then and surely not now.

She surprised me when she chuckled softly. "Seems like our roles have reversed."

"Never that."

She nodded, her face expressionless. "Allure, you feel I took something from you?"

I continued to stare her down. "Yes. I do."

"I feel the same."

I narrowed my eyes at her, confused.

"You stole his heart from me years ago. You know, we have a big house. It is beautiful. And we have the most adorable boys. A picture-perfect life. And still he is not happy. He does not love me. But I love him. I have always, always loved him. Even when I shouldn't have. Even when he wasn't mine. And I was never bothered by the fact that he wasn't mine, just as long as I could have some part of him. But now he is mine. And I don't plan on letting him go. Ever."

I looked away. She had never cared that she had assisted in breaking up my home. What did this bitch expect to get out of this conversation? An apology?

"I'm not fucking James."

"Yet or not anymore?"

"Listen, in my mind I have a whole lot of things I want to say to you. But that would be stating the obvious. My eyes fully tell how I feel about you. But let's get shit straight. *You* made a decision to fuck with James when you knew he was with me. So I could give a shit about your sentiment or your pain. I really can't do anything for you. This conversation should be had with your husband, if he is doing some shit you don't approve of, it's not with me. I don't have shit to say to you. I didn't then, and I don't now. Fuck your feelings."

But I knew I was really lying to myself. I did feel guilty.

"You know this could get ugly, don't you?"

I sized her up with my eyes, shook my head, and chuckled. "You know what? I think this conversation is over. Because if I am not mistaken, I could swear you just threatened me. Lady, I'm a survivor from the east side of Long Beach. Can't a motherfucking person or thing break me. You, on the other hand, best be careful. You don't seem like you strong enough for war."

She stared me down. I did the same to her, letting her know I wasn't playing with her ass. If she was coming for me, I was going to meet her ass halfway.

She nodded, as if I had convinced her not to fuck with me, and her face softened. Mine didn't.

"In all actuality. I don't owe you an explanation any more than you felt you owed me one three years ago," I told her. "But yes, I did sleep with James once since you've been married. But I won't again. There. Are we done?"

She kept her poker face on. But I knew it was probably tearing her up inside that I had confessed to sleeping with James. Still, no sort of emotion showed on her face.

When I left her at that picnic table to walk to my car, my mind tried to process what had just transpired between James's wife and me. And exactly what to do about it. I understood how she felt, only because I was once her. So while I related, at the same time, I thought the bitch had some nerve. She had done the same thing to me, and yet she had the nerve to confront me. I felt bad and outraged at the same damn time.

Chapter 13

When I got to Sierra's game, I tried to stay calm and to focus, but I knew I had to tell James what had gone down. I waited until halftime. James and I walked outside to the parking lot.

"What's up, baby?"

"Your wife came to my job."

His eyes widened. "What?"

"Don't act like—"

'Baby, I swear I didn't know. A couple times she asked me if was sleeping with you, and I told her no. But I did tell her I was in Sierra's life. She didn't like it. But I told her to accept it, bottom line."

"I really shouldn't care if this affects your marriage, because of what you and she both put me through, but I do. Maybe it's better if you—"

"Allure, stop. Don't even say it. I promised Sierra and I'm going to keep that promise and that's it. I told my wife we not fucking, and that's the truth. For my sacrifices in this marriage, I really don't give a fuck if she don't like it."

"That's your wife."

"You are too nice. Why you care about how she feels?"

"It's the right thing to do, that's why. I realize that she didn't care about that back then, and neither did you."

"I know, baby. I fucked up. But what I am telling you is that this is going to stay the way it is. I'm in Sierra's life, period."

I wasn't so sure anymore if this was a good idea. I was just about to mention how she had threatened me when my cell phone rang.

James's eyes were glued to my phone as I checked the caller ID and then answered. It was Christopher.

"Hi, Chris."

James frowned and looked away.

"Hey, baby. You were on my mind, so I'm reaching out."

"Awww. Thanks."

"You want to hit a flick later tonight?"

"Maybe. Give me a few minutes and I will call you back."

"Okay. Bye, babe."

I ended the call.

"Is that the dude you been seeing? You seem more serious than you admitted to."

"James!"

"Listen. I love you. Still. But even though I love you, Allure, I want you to have happiness."

Although I liked Chris, I sometimes felt—no, I knew—I was still in love with James, and his coming around wasn't making it any better. It was actually resurrecting my desire to be with him.

"Last question. Say, hypothetically, that my marriage failed, I got a divorce within the year, and I was single. Would you give me another chance?"

I gasped at what he was saying. It made my heart skip a beat. I turned my back to him. And that part of me that had wanted this man back for so long, for so many years after he had left me, was singing at what he had just asked me. That ray of hope I had suppressed for so long was no longer suppressed. I was sure James saw the look of long-ing on my face. Tears started running down my cheeks. For so long all I had ever wanted was for him to leave her and come back to me the right way. Was he offering me that now for real? I wasn't sure. My uncertainty scared the shit out of me. Because he could, after all, just be giving me false hope, like he had many times before. So I forced myself not to believe what he had said. He was making my anxiety level go up by the second.

James turned me back around to face him. He lifted my chin with one of his hands. "Why are you crying, baby?" Then, before I could stop him, he started kissing me.

I allowed myself to get caught up in the moment, and I didn't stop him, despite all the warning sounds going off in my head. I kissed him back, despite the fact that I had said I would never let him touch me again. I was hungrily kissing him back.

He paused in the midst of the kissing and said, "I love you." Then he explored my lips again with his own, invading the inside of my mouth with his tongue, then teasing my tongue with his.

"You lying, cheating bastard!"

My eyes popped open just in time to see James's wife coming our way in a fury. James shoved me out of the way and turned around. His wife started punching him with closed fists, crying and yelling as she did.

"Latasha, stop!" James shouted. He grabbed both her arms with his hands.

"You're a liar!" she screamed between her sobs.

I stood there, frozen, as she struggled against him.

"You bitch! I'm going to make you pay!" she yelled at me.

"Latasha, stop!" James shouted at her again.

"No!" She continued to cry loudly.

James gave me one last look before damn near dragging her to his car.

I looked around, relieved that no one else was in the parking lot. Still shaken up, I watched James put her in his car. Then he ran over to the driver's side, hopped in, and skidded out of the parking lot. I walked back into the gym, thinking that this was déjà vu. This was just like the day I was pregnant and caught them in the act in James's truck. It felt like that day, but now our roles were reversed. How crazy was that? As I had watched James's wife cry, I had felt bad for her. And at the same time I had felt dumb for feeling bad for her, because she hadn't cared about the fact that she had fucked James when I was with him, and thus had hurt me.

"Mom, are you okay?" Sierra asked me as we walked up the steps to our house. I knew she was asking me this because I had been quiet the whole way home, and although I had tried to cover my face with my hand, I knew she had seen a few tears fall.

"I'm okay." I grabbed the mail and unlocked the door.

Once we slipped inside, I sat my things down so I could go through the mail. Sierra shrugged at me and went into her room. Thoughts of what had just happened with James, me, and his wife flashed through my head.

"Sierra!" I called.

She ran back in the living room. "Yeah, Mom?"

"I'm not up to cooking, and I'm not hungry, so make a frozen pizza."

"Sounds good to me!" She went into the kitchen, and I scanned the mail. There was a light bill and Sierra's *American Girl Italiza Magazine* bill. The rest was junk mail.

Sierra came back into the living room. "Mom, you dropped this one."

She handed me an envelope. I scanned it. It was from my doctor's office. I opened it quickly. The letter simply said that they had been trying to contact me and to call them to schedule an appointment. I grabbed my cordless phone and called the office. I had not missed a phone call from them.

"Dr. Patel's office."

"Hi. This is Allure Jones. I got a letter saying you guys needed me to call you."

"Yes. The doctor wanted to go over your exam results. The number we have on file says it is no longer in service."

I remembered that when Sierra and I got the Samsung phones, I had changed my number.

"Oh, I'm sorry. I changed my number a few months ago and forgot to update you."

"Okay. What is your new number?"

I gave it to the receptionist.

"Okay. Well, the doctor wants you to come in for your annual results. We have an opening tomorrow at eleven forty-five, three thirty, or five thirty."

Just then my line clicked. It was James. I ignored it.

"Three thirty."

"Okay, we will see you then."

Just as I ended the call, Chris called. I was too shaken up to talk to him. I knew I was still in love with James. I liked Chris. And yes, I felt bad about Latasha's pain, despite the fact that she had never felt bad about any of mine.

I called Creole and explained what had happened. I knew she wouldn't judge but would give me solid advice.

"Well, Allure, I tell you, at first I was happy with the arrangement. James was coming around for Sierra. But what kills me is the bitch had the nerve to get mad after what she did."

"I know. Nonetheless, I can't gloat in her face and feel good about where we are now, that I fucked her husband. I feel bad for her."

"That's because you are a good person, Allure. You have always been too damn good for your own good. But don't waste time you can't get back by stressing about that bitch's feelings. Fuck her. But in dealing with James, go by your morals."

"You know what James asked me? He asked me, if he were to leave her, would I take him back?"

"And you said, 'Fuck no,' right?"

"I didn't say anything. Thing is, I still do love James. And I want—"

"Don't say it! When it comes to him, I just don't think any good will come your way. What good can come from him being back in your life? For Sierra, cool. And you have a decent man in your life. Why not give that a chance?"

I listened to Creole for a few more minutes. She was right. James and his track record were not good at all. Why give him another chance to screw me over?

"But whatever decision you make, I will always be here for you. And whatever happens, you have my support."

"Thanks, Creole."

After ending the call, I popped two Motrin PM and went to bed.

Chapter 14

The next morning Sierra and I headed to my car so I could drop her off and go to school. As we walked to my car, I saw that I had been hit with another blow. My car had been vandalized. It was like someone had taken a razor and gone into a wild frenzy, keying up my car. And all my tires were slashed.

Sierra gasped.

"Go to the neighbors and get a ride with them. I'm gonna get you after practice," I told her.

"Okay." She ran off.

I then called the police and requested that someone come out to take a report. In my mind I knew who had done this. James's wife.

Then I called James.

"What's up, baby?"

"Get over here now!"

Funny thing was, as I waited for the police to come, James got there first. I knew it was because my misfortune wasn't a top priority for the police. As I waited, I asked myself if I could really be mad. Did I have that right? What if Latasha had never had any type of involvement with James? Would it have made a difference? Did it make it better that James's wife was once his mistress? Was it still fucked up even if I had slept with him? Was what she did to my car justified?

James pulled into my driveway, hopped out of his car without even glancing at mine, and rushed over to me. "What happened?"

I said nothing, just pointed to my car.

He finally looked at it, and then I watched him throw a distressed look my way before walking over to my car. He walked around it slowly. He stood there for a moment before walking back up to me.

"Who—"

"James, don't fucking play with me. You know damn well your wife did this shit."

He took a deep breath. "Yeah, well, she gave me pure hell last night, after catching us kissing."

"If anyone can relate to her pain, it's me. But you . . . You created this shit, James, three years ago."

He said nothing, just looked at me.

"The police are on their way."

His eyes widened. "What? No, Allure."

"What do you mean, no? She fucked up my car, James. She told me the day we met that this could get ugly."

"But she is my wife. You can't let my sons' mother go to jail. Baby, please don't tell them anything about my wife."

"How can you ask me not to do that shit?"

"Because if it were you, I wouldn't let her—"

"Oh, I doubt that. You have never protected me. You spared me no pain with the dirty shit you did."

"I know, but I will pay for all the damages. If you tell them, she will lose her job and—"

"And what?"

"Come on, baby. Just do what I ask. When the police come, don't tell them anything about my wife."

When the police finally came and took a report, I left out everything about his wife. I didn't even mention the fact that she had been pretty much stalking me and had threatened me, because of the guilt trip that James had laid on me about the mother of his kids going to jail. True to his word, James had my car towed to the shop of my choosing and completely repaired. He even paid for a rental car for me until my car was ready to be picked up.

***

Since I had called off work due to my vandalized car, I simply used the day to run errands. I even remembered I needed to stop by my doctor's office.

As I waited in one of the examination rooms, my anxiety level was high because of that bitch Latasha. Would she stop? What would she try to do next? James had assured me that he would talk to her and scare her into leaving me alone for good, but who really knew? He had said for me just to trust him and he would fix this.

I texted Creole and told her what had gone down. She was in utter shock.

Her response was, So are we going to go fuck her up?

No. I'm going to let James deal with it.

That bitch is really crazy.

Before I could respond, a call from Kendra came through. I sent it to voice mail. For the first time in our friendship, I felt I couldn't open up to Kendra about a situation. I had, after all, slept with a married man, and Kendra was married. What would she think of me? Just then the doctor walked into the room.

"Hello, Allure."

"Hey, Renee." We were cool, so I always called her by her first name. I had been going to her ever since I joined the school district.

"How are things?" She scanned my chart.

"Good."

"You don't sound so sure. Are you okay?"

I offered a fake smile. "I am."

"And Sierra?"

"Always good."

"Good." She stared at me for a moment. "Your blood work is fine. Your pelvic exam was good. However, I don't know the best way to tell you this, but your galactogram, which we used to determine what the discharge was, tested positive for a breast mass." She closed her eyes briefly before saying, "Allure, the mass is malignant."

I gasped. "What?" I needed her to repeat herself, because I started to have trouble breathing from the panic.

"You have breast cancer, Allure. I'm so, so sorry."

So am I, I thought.

When I looked in her eyes, they were watery, and as I cried on the examination table, she cried tears with me. All I was thinking was, how could this happen to me now? After I had everything in my life in order. I started sobbing.

She walked over to me and hugged me. For a long time she just held me, and then she said, "It is going to be okay. You have options, and never forget you are a survivor."

I wiped my tear-soaked face and nodded.

She took the time to explain what my options were. I would have to get my breast removed, go through chemotherapy and possibly radiation. She said for some women, it could be fatal, and some ended up cancer free. My cell phone started ringing. It was James. I ignored it. I had all these scary thoughts about my diagnosis in my head. Would I be around for my daughter? I continued to ask myself. Yeah, Renee had said that some survived . . . but some didn't. Which one would I be? It was not like I had a choice. It was what God's will was. And His will could be life or it could be death. My phone continued to ring. I turned it off.

After Renee went over everything, she gave me a date to start my chemo. I then left the office. On the way home I had to pull the car over twice because I couldn't stop crying. I cried like a baby. I was so fucking scared.

As Sierra and I sat down for dinner, I knew she could tell that there was something wrong with me. I tried to keep a poker face, but she saw how quiet I was. And I had got us both McDonald's, but I had no appetite.

"Mommy, are you okay?"

"My head hurts, is all."

"You want some aspirin?"

"No. But I'm going to go lie down."

"Okay. But do you want me to bring you something to drink?" She was such a caring kid.

"No. Thank you."

As I got up to go to my bedroom, she said, "Mom, James texted me and said for you to call him."

"Okay." But instead I went to sleep.

Chapter 15

The next day I went to my job and informed them that I had breast cancer and I needed to take a leave of absence. I was set to start my chemo in a week. They offered to let me leave that day, but I told them I wanted to stay and then take the rest of the week off to get things in order for my treatments. They understood. It made me so sad. It was hard to tell all my students that I would be gone for some months. A lot of them looked at me like I was their mother. Several of my students broke down crying in the class. It was just not easy. But I assured them I would be back.

The next day Christopher called me repeatedly, and even Kendra left me a few messages, asking me what was going on with me and why I wasn't responding to Chris. I called him and told him I was just super busy. The holidays were coming up and I was doing conferences was the excuse I gave. He accepted it. Now, I knew James, on the other hand, wouldn't just lie down and accept that his calls were being ignored for a couple days. One day, as I prepared to step out to pick Sierra up from school, he was on my doorstep.

Before I could say anything, he blurted, "What's going on, baby? I been calling you for three days, and you won't respond."

"I know. I—"

"Can I come in?"

I stepped aside and let him enter. Once I closed the door and turned to face him, he grabbed me, swung me in the air, and kissed me on my lips. I tried to pull away.

"James! Put me down."

He did but kept his arms curved around my waist. "Baby, I came to tell you some good news." He pulled me over to the couch, sat down, then sat me on his lap. For a moment he just stared at me.

Shyly, I looked away but asked, "Why are you looking at me like that?"

"Because you are just so pretty to me, baby." He kissed me on my lips, and the fire I had felt in the parking lot ignited within me.

"Listen, my grandfather passed. I'm flying out there to make sure my mother is okay and to help her with the funeral arrangements. And I want you to come with me."

"James, I—"

He put a finger to my lips. "I'm filing for divorce."

I looked at him, surprised. I was not expecting him to say that.

"Bring Sierra, and we can get away from all of this and start a new life. Knowing you, you're probably worried about my sons, but you don't have to worry. I am going to get joint custody. They will be with their mother half the year and with me the other half. She can't prevent me from seeing my kids as long as I pay child support. What do you say, baby? I know there will be a little adjustment, but we will all adjust."

A few days ago I would have been positively elated about what he had just offered me. It was something I had been longing for, for such a long, long time. But . . . Knowing what I knew about my breast cancer, I couldn't let him do this, couldn't let him leave his wife. What if I were to die in six months and he broke up his family to be with me? That would be selfish. But I didn't want to tell him this, about the cancer. I didn't want him to feel obligated to be with me. I wanted him to do the right thing by his kids. Although it was scary to say I might not be here for much longer, I had to accept the fact that there was a big possibility that I wouldn't. As much as I loved this man—and, boy, did I love him—I couldn't do it.

"I can't just leave my job."

"Baby, Louisiana has teaching jobs. And in all actuality, you know I got money. I don't really have to work. I never did. I just chose to, to stay out of trouble. You don't have to work, either, if you don't want to. You can stay home and raise my kids and take care of me."

"So what are you offering me the opportunity to be?"

"My wife. When my divorce clears, I will give you the wedding of your dreams. Because if I didn't learn shit in these three years, I learned that I love you, baby. With all that's in me to love. I want you by my side indefinitely."

I was crumbling inside. But I had to do this. I had to end this. I couldn't let him divorce his wife and leave his kids for me.

"James. I can't. I'm pregnant," I blurted, hoping that would be it.

If looks could kill, his would have. He gave me a hateful look and shoved me off of him. I stood and faced him. He stood as well.

"Wait. I don't think I heard you right." He looked infuriated.

"You heard me." I walked a few feet away from him and turned my back.

"Come here."

"No! You heard me."

He walked up to me and spun me around to face him. That was when his face crumbled. He started shaking me, all while his tears flowed and wouldn't stop flowing. "How could you do this to me, baby? You knew! You know how much I love you! I told you I would fix this—"

"It's too late to fix!" I was crying too. "I don't love you anymore."

"You're fucking lying, Allure!"

"No, I'm not. I'm three months."

His eyes widened. He released me and wiped his face. Then, for a moment, he just looked at me like he wanted to slap the shit out of me. Silence was all he gave me. Then he walked to the door, gave me one final look. A sob escaped his throat, though he tried to muffle it. His shoulders shuddered, and then he left my home. I broke down crying on the couch. I had just given up the chance to have the man I had loved for so long. He had promised me my dreams. Marriage, the opportunity to spend the rest of my life with him. But I might not have a life to live. This cancer could positively destroy me, and it was too much of a gamble for James to break up his home, leave his kids. I knew I had made the right choice, although the shit hurt like hell.

Before I started my chemo, I cooked a dinner of rib eye steaks, homemade macaroni and cheese, mashed potatoes, string beans, and a three-layer lemon–cream-cheese-cake. I invited my mother, Creole, and Kendra over and told them I had some news to share with them. I knew it would be really hard to tell them all, especially Sierra, that I had breast cancer. But I had to. Bottom line.

After we ate everything but dessert, saving it for later, we went into the living room to sit down. Apprehension filled me as I contemplated how to tell them all properly about my cancer. I mean, how would they take it? Sierra was only nine years old, and I was the only real parent she had. I think I would have positively cracked if my mother had told me when I was nine years old that she had cancer. And my mother had already lost one child. I knew the most important thing I had to convey to them, whether I believed it or not, was that I was going to be okay. And I didn't believe it. But I wasn't going to let them know that.

"You said you had some news for us, right, Allure? What is it? Did Chris propose to you?" Kendra asked.

I laughed. "I haven't really been seeing him lately."

"Why not? Allure, if you let this good man—"

"I have breast cancer," I blurted. Then I closed my eyes briefly, took a deep breath, glad I had finally said it. I was greeted with silence. When I opened my eyes, I was met with four sets of wide eyes.

"Allure," Kendra said evenly, "What did you say?"

"I said I have breast cancer."

"Oh, my God!" That was my mother.

Sierra started crying and ran out of the room. Creole went after her.

Within a matter of seconds my mom was hiding her face in her forearm on the couch and sobbing. Tears were slipping down Kendra's face. Before I could stand to check on Sierra, she and Creole walked back into the living room. Creole had her arm around Sierra. They both sat back down across from me. Creole didn't cry. I had never seen her cry. But she did go off.

"Why in the fuck!" She shook her head. "Why in the fuck does bad stuff have to always happen to you? I don't get this shit!"

"Creole, I'm going to be okay. I am going to have my left breast removed. I am going to do the chemo too. I'll undergo it as many times as I need to, to survive this shit." I turned to my daughter. "Sierra I know you're scared, but if you don't know nothing else, know your mother was born a fighter. And ain't shit on this earth going to take me away from you."

"Okay," Sierra said, wiping her teary eyes.

My mother's shoulders were shaking uncontrollably. I knew what she was thinking: she had lost one child, and she just might lose another. But I was not going to just lie down and voluntarily die. That didn't mean I wasn't going to die. I very well might. But I was going to try my best not to let that happen. In all honesty, I was just as scared and worried as they were. But I wasn't going to show it. I had to give them hope. I didn't want them worrying about me. *What will be will be.* None of us knew what the outcome would be. I didn't want them all stressing and spending their days depressed over me. So I kept up a brave front.

"Ma, don't worry. And I am going to need all your help and support. Mom, while I go through chemo, I need Sierra to stay with you."

After I went over the treatment and the amount of time I would be in the hospital, and I answered all the questions everyone had, they offered me their support.

"I'll get Sierra on the weekends," Creole offered.

"And whatever you need, let me know," Kendra said.

I smiled. I had expected this to be harder, but I thought that because I took a "failure is not an option" type of attitude around them, they calmed down and they adopted the same type of mentality. Did I really feel that way? Hell, no. I had never been so scared. But I kept a smile on my face.

"Okay. We're good, then." I stood. "Now let's go eat some cake."

Chapter 16

After phone call after phone call I agreed to meet Chris for dinner at Gladstone's at The Pike. My plan was simply to tell him I couldn't see him anymore. With me about to get one of my breasts removed, I was in no real condition to date anyone. Even if he was a nice guy.

When I got there, he was already seated. He stood when he saw me.

"Hey, beautiful."

"Hi."

He walked from around his side of the table and gave me a hug and a kiss on my cheek. Then he pulled out my chair for me. I smiled and knew this would be harder than I thought, especially with him being so sweet. I mean, I did like Chris

"Thanks." I sat down, and he scooted my chair up.

"So how have you been?" he asked, sitting back down across from me.

"Okay, and you?"

"Missing you."

I looked away at that comment. It made me feel bad. He had shown a genuine interest in me, and I was doing him like this. And it was more than just the cancer. It was the fact that I had one foot in and one foot out of something with James emotionally.

The waitress came, and we placed our orders. He ordered crab cakes for us to share, and jerk salmon, rice and veggies himself. I ordered lobster mac and cheese.

"Allure, I really like you and—"

"Why?"

"Because you're fine, baby, sweet, hardworking, and I'm sure there is more, but you won't give me a chance to see that more."

I rolled my eyes.

He studied my angry-looking expression. "Why so harsh, baby?"

"Because I don't know what you want."

"I want you. I want to see you more, take you out, make you smile. Why don't you believe that?"

"Because I have heard this a dozen times. And what you niggas tend to do instead is pass through."

He was silent. So was I. There was a lot of tension at the table, of which I was the creator. He hadn't come here to pick a fight. I knew this. But I had to push this man away.

"I thought you and I were getting somewhere. I didn't know you still had your reservations about me. Kendra said you are like a sister to her. You'd have to know she would not fix you up with someone who is just about hurting you. I'm not that man."

When the food came out, despite how good it smelled, I really couldn't enjoy it. It had been like that ever since I found out I had breast cancer. I ate a few bites before shoving my dish away, and I had not even tasted the crab cakes, which came out before our entrées did.

"Babe, what can I do to prove that I am for all things good when it comes to my intentions toward you?"

Okay. I was done with the bitch farce. I took a deep breath. "Look, I'm just going through something really hard, and if I tell you what it is, you aren't going to want to deal with me, trust me."

"I'm a real man all day. Noth—"

"I have breast cancer. Pretty soon, in a matter of days, I'm going to be walking around with one titty and no hair. And after all of that, I still might die. Could you deal with that?"

"Yes."

My head snapped back, and my eyes were bugged out. Was this man crazy, or was he just so curious about how my coochie felt that he was saying this?

"Lord Jesus, what do you want? What is your game?"

"I'm not buying the attitude. I know it's not you."

"What do you want, Chris, for real?"

"To be there for you. Seems like you spend all your time caring about others. For once let someone care about Allure."

"You're not going to go through with what you're saying, Chris. I'm not going to let you set me up for disappointment." My fear came back to me. In two more days my breast would be removed, and I was scared as hell. I started crying. And he came around from his side of the table and, despite the stares, got on his knees and held me in the restaurant.

"Let me show you, baby. That's all I ask."

"I'm so scared, Chris, so scared. But yes, I do need someone to be there for me." And he let me sob on his shoulder.

After healing from my breast being removed, I didn't have time to miss it, since I started the chemo. It lasted about five weeks and kicked my ass. I was always nauseated, so I wouldn't eat much, and I was always constipated. So I was a miserable soldier. And yes, I lost all my hair. Every bit of it. It fell out during my chemo treatments. Every bit of hair I had on my body. I didn't even have eyebrows. The doctors said it would grow back approximately ten months after my chemo treatments were done. I had to wait another month after chemo for my radiation. Usually, you did it for five to six weeks, but my doctor had me do it for four.

I had so much support from my mother, Sierra, Creole, Kendra, and Chris. Let's just say that this man never seemed to leave my side. In fact, after work and every single day off he had, he was in a chair next to me in the hospital, despite me being bald and all and having only one titty. The shit was crazy to me. I had never had a man care for me like that. It was crazy.

He was even there my first day back home. Since my doctor said it would take me another two months to recover and return to my normal self after the therapy, Sierra stayed with my mother. And Chris took a leave of absence to take care of me. I told him he shouldn't have done it, but he insisted. Lord, that man. The recovery process was difficult, and it was hard for me to do the normal things I used to be able to do. I would have hand cramps, coordination problems, and thinking difficulties. Sometimes I couldn't walk more than three steps without feeling dizzy. And I was fatigued, extremely fatigued, to the point where I stayed in bed most of the day and slept. Chris did the cleaning and cooking.

On this day he said he was going to make some chili. I was looking forward to it because as I was getting my strength back, my appetite was coming back as well.

I had just jumped out of the shower, wrapped a towel around myself, and gone back in my room to throw on a dress. The hardest thing for me aside from the cancer and losing my hair was looking at my now deformed body. My only option to fix it was cosmetic surgery. I looked away from the mirror in disgust. Aside from my breast being gone and the ugly scar, I had lost so much shapeliness. I was stick skinny. My doctor had said I would gain it all back. I hoped I did.

"Hey, baby, the chili is done."

I looked in my mirror and saw Chris's head peek in my door, which was slightly ajar.

His eyes widened when he saw me nude. "I'm sorry."

"What are you doing?" I demanded, throwing a towel over myself.

"I . . ." He stepped away from the door.

I pulled on a nightgown, instantly feeling bad. It was my fault I had left my door open, so I couldn't blame him. And the truth was, I was just embarrassed that he had seen my disfigurement.

I took a deep breath and went into the kitchen. He was seated, eating a bowl of chili. There was another bowl on the table, which was filled with chili and sprinkled with cheese, green onions, and diced tomato. His chili had the same garnishes and what looked like sour cream on it. I hated sour cream. He had even made corn bread.

We both ate in silence, a very awkward silence, because our meals were always filled with conversation.

After a few minutes he asked, "How is the chili?"

"I'm sorry, Chris." Tears started gliding down my face. "I just . . . I didn't want you to see me nude. I'm just so ugly. I didn't want you to see it."

He laid his spoon in his bowl and stood to his feet. "Come here, Allure."

I stood to my feet as well. He grabbed me by one of my hands and gently guided me back into my bedroom. He placed me in front of my mirror and stood behind me.

"Just trust me, baby. Relax." Before I could stop him, he pulled my nightgown over my head.

I closed my eyes in shame as I stood nude before him. Tears burned under my lids. How would I ever be able to be with a man again if I felt this way? I'd always have the scar.

"Open your eyes," he said.

I did, and tears ran down my cheeks.

"What do you see?"

"A freak. My body is disfigured. There is a long, ugly scar, and I'm skin and bones." I wiped my tears away. "What do you see?"

"What I saw from day one, a beautiful woman."

"Stop, Chris! No man could possibly think I'm beautiful. You don't have to feel sorry for me and lie to my face. You don't have to feel obligated to still be here, Chris. You' re not an ugly man. There are plenty of women that would love a man like you."

"I'm not worried about other women. And, Allure, it's important that you understand that I'm here because I want to be. I'm still here because I love you."

I blinked rapidly. "What?"

"I love you. It's because I love you that I still see you the way I see you and I still desire you the way I desired you before the cancer. When you love a person, you love them unconditionally. Well, at least I do."

It was funny that he had said that. Thing was, when it came to men, I never felt that they were able to do this with me. I loved Greg and James unconditionally, despite their flaws and fuckups, but they never gave me the same courtesy.

He stared at me in the mirror. "I mean it, Allure. I'm in love with you. And I know you been hurt, baby. That's not my plan . . . to give you more hurt. All I want is to make you and Sierra happy. Be what no man has ever been to you. So you can beat me up, try to push me away, or talk all the shit you want, babe, but I'm not going nowhere."

"Why?"

He chuckled and wrapped his arms around my naked body. "So many reasons. I already told you that you're beautiful, you're smart, sweet, funny, a critical thinker, and you're not disillusioned about reality. You're a good mother and overall a good person. You just have that spark. What is there not to like about you? See, you can't believe my words, because you have been with men who tore you down instead of building you up. I have no problem building you back up, baby."

He turned me to face him, and then he lifted up my face and started kissing me gently. His hands stroked up and down my back. This was my first kiss since James. I enjoyed kissing Chris. He picked me up and carried me to my bed. My heart skipped a beat when he joined me on the bed.

"Lay back, baby. I want to make you feel good."

"Okay."

He started kissing me all over. My neck, collarbone, breast, even my scar. While he kissed on my body, his hand massaged my pussy, making me moan. He had thick fingers, and they stroked in and out of me, making squishing sounds because of my wetness. Then, suddenly, he sat up, spread my legs wide, made a fist with his hand, and started using quick jerking motions up and down my shaft, from my clit to the end of my vaginal opening. It truly was a pleasure that I had never experienced before. I held my legs up as he took me to some major heights. I moaned over and over again as he did this relentlessly! Before I could stop myself, I squirted a hot liquid. But that didn't stop him.

He kept going over and over again, and fluid continued to spurt out of me. Then, when I thought I couldn't take any more, he went down on me. He had his tongue pressed flat against my clit. The sensations felt so good. He alternated between my opening and my clit, sliding his tongue up and down. I moaned in ecstasy, grabbing one of his hands, the one that was pressed flat against the bed.

"Please, Chris," I begged.

He continued to tease me before standing to his feet and taking off his clothes. As he stood naked in front of me, my eyes raked up and down his body. It was freaking beautiful. And his dick hung like a damn tree trunk. He was huge. He slid a condom on and straddled me. He slipped inside my wetness. I held on to his back and moaned loudly.

He stared down at me. "You look sexy when you make that face, and I like the way you moan," he whispered in a husky voice. He started going inside of me. "Damn, it feels so good being inside of you," he said.

He sped up the pace. His lips were now on mine and I tasted myself and I didn't mind. He flipped on his back and lifted me on top of him. His hands glided down to my hips, and he controlled my movements. One of his fingers played with my clit. He rubbed it back and forth as I rode him. It felt so good gliding up and down on him. His hands went back to my waist, and he gripped me and slammed me up and down on him, causing me to take him all the way inside of me. The motions were too much for me, and I laid my head on his chest, convulsing.

After our lovemaking, Chris brought me my bowl of chili and fed it to me in bed. As he spooned chili into my mouth, I thought about my situation. I had finally allowed someone to sleep with me besides James. I knew James had moved on from me three years ago, but I hadn't let go of the idea of him. And now I had. To a certain degree, the aftermath felt funny.

"Where do we go from here?" I asked Chris.

"Where do you want to go from here?"

I laughed. "Why don't you just answer my question?"

"Sorry. Let's see. I'd like you to be my wife, Allure." Then he placed another spoonful of chili in my mouth.

I damn near choked on it. I knew he didn't just say that. I had assumed he'd say, "More sex, maybe go steady," but not what he said, no, no, no.

"You heard me correctly," he said, as if reading my thoughts. "I don't know why you think I'm playing. Little boys play. That's what you been dealing with. Well, I'm all man all day. And with me there is no confusion or indecision. I always know what I want and what's right for me. If you're still scared and you need me to spend more time with you, that is fine. Eventually, you will see that I am here to stay. I won't disappoint you. I waited for you this long, Allure. I'll wait longer, because for a woman like you, it's worth it."

I punked the game yet again, because I started crying again over his words.

He leaned over and kissed me, then whispered in my ear, "I'm here to stay."

Chapter 17

I finally accepted Chris in my heart after we made love. He never wavered on all the things he had said he would do. He was still coming around consistently. I had started back at work, and so had he. But that didn't stop him from calling me, coming over, tending to my needs, and taking me out wherever my heart desired to go. Then James came back.

Since it was still taking time for my hair to grow back, I was wearing a wig. I had several different ones, ranging in color from jet black to sandy brown. I named my jet-black one Sasha Fierce, my sandy-colored one Grace Kelly, and my reddish-colored one Big Red. And the thing with the wigs was that they were hotter than a motha.

What made it worse on this day was the fact that I was in the kitchen, frying chicken wings. It was hot enough as it was in a wig and ever hotter when you frying something. So I took off my wig and sat it on the kitchen table. Sierra and Chris had both seen me in my baldness, so they weren't tripping. I smiled, thinking about Chris. I had been so blessed to meet a man like him. He had been so supportive of me throughout this whole experience.

I flipped the chicken over. It was smelling really good. That was when I heard my doorbell ring.

"Sierra! See who it is," I called. But she had her bedroom door closed. I hated when she did that.

I sighed, walked to the front door, and peered through the peephole. My heart started beating wildly. It was

James! Six months had passed since I had seen him last. I wondered when he had come back to California. I always assumed he had kept his word and left because I never heard from or saw him again.

I panicked. What would I tell him about the baby if he asked? To keep up the lie, I knew that I could say that I had had a miscarriage or that I had had the baby prematurely. Who knew that I would still be here and that the cancer would be completely gone? My doctors had been hopeful that I would be cancer free due to the fact that they had caught it so early.

I rushed back into the kitchen and grabbed my wig. The doorbell rang again. I pulled my wig on quickly, not bothering to snap the combs on.

I ran back to the living room, took a deep breath, and opened the front door.

When we were face-to-face, James offered me a smile. "Hey. Can I come in?"

"Sure."

I stepped back and let him enter. Once he did, I turned to walk to Sierra's room and let her know James was there. "Let me get Sierra."

He gently grabbed one of my arms. "No. Wait. I want to talk to you for a moment."

I smoothed my wig down, hoping it didn't slip off any, and pulled my arm back. "Talk," I snapped.

He frowned. "You haven't seen me in well over six months, and that's how you come at me? Why all the anger, Allure?"

"Here you go. I'm not about to kiss your ass because you popped back up."

"Allure, I wasn't asking you to do that but . . . Hell, I can't help it if I miss you still and needed to see your face. "

"I don't want to hear this." I turned to walk away. He grabbed my arm again, this time more firmly. I snatched it away with all my might. "Let me go, god—"

He gasped, and his eyes became wide. My wig had slipped halfway off. Before I could adjust it, James stepped closer to me and pulled it completely off. I started crying instantly, ashamed that he saw it, my bald head. I covered my mouth with my hand and felt tears of humiliation slip out of my eyes.

"What happened to you?" he whispered, horrified.

I turned away from him and didn't respond.

He turned me back around to face him. "Baby?" He grabbed my shoulders. "You not going to get away from me until you tell me what happened to all your hair."

I took a deep breath. "I was never pregnant. I lied. I had just found out that I had breast cancer. That is why my hair fell out. Chemo made me lose my hair, James."

"What? Why didn't you tell me, baby?" As he spoke, his eyes welled up with tears and he broke down sobbing, all while shaking the shit out of me. "Why didn't you tell me, baby? Why didn't you let me be there for you?" He dropped to his knees and held my waist. He buried his face in it and continued crying, crying like a baby. It made me cry as well.

A few minutes, later I sat across from James on the couch.

His eyes were red from crying, and his voice was hoarse. "I just wish you had told me. I would have never left. I would have stayed. Baby, I would have taken care of you and Sierra. You wouldn't have had to go through this alone. I hate that you were alone."

"James, I wasn't. I had my family, friends, Sierra, and Chris."

His jealously was instant. "So you were still seeing him?"

"He never left my side."

He looked so hurt when I said that. "Allure, I wouldn't have left your side, either. But you didn't give me the chance to prove that to you."

"I didn't want to be selfish with you. There was always a chance that I wouldn't make it. And I didn't want to hurt your boys by breaking up their home."

"You would have never been responsible for that. I started this mess long ago with my fucking around and marrying a woman I didn't love. I married her for the wrong reasons. So I was the one that needed to fix this."

"Okay."

He said, "I would have been there for you."

"I'm sorry for hurting you."

He looked away. "Just so you know, I did file for divorce. I stayed away for the time that I did because I couldn't bear to see you carrying someone else's baby. Just the thought of it crushed me. But, Allure, you don't know how many times I rehearsed in my head so many different scenarios of that day I came to tell you the news. Seems like all of them were more desirable than what actually went down. I thought you would run into my arms and kiss me and give me that look you used to give me. You remember that day I called you from the office and you were feeding Jeremiah? You remember what you told me?"

I shook my head.

"You told me that waking up to me was like waking up to Superman." He chuckled. "You said you felt like I came home, hung up my suit and cape in the closet, and climbed into bed with you. I never told you, but all that day you had me walking around with my chest out. And when I would come home, before I could even get my key in the door, here you came, rushing out and hugging me like I had been gone for so long. Back then I took these small things for granted. But I honestly would have killed for you to look at me like that again. I thought that was how you were going to look at me when I told you that finally I was going to do the right thing by you. But I guess I was hoping for just too much." He looked really troubled.

Just then Sierra ran into the room.

"James!" she said excitedly. She threw herself in his arms.

"Hey, pretty girl."

Sierra chopped it up with James ecstatically, telling him how her basketball season went, how her grades were, and about her friends. He listened intently.

I watched them together for a second, and then I went into the kitchen to finish cooking dinner. Later James joined us at the dinner table, and it was awkward as hell. But since Sierra continued to run her mouth, it took away some of the awkwardness. As she talked, my mind was working. James was finally a single man. And yet I now had a man who really cared for me. Was it worth giving up Chris for James? What if James cheated or hurt me again?

After dinner Sierra very conveniently went off to her room to study. But I knew she was doing this so she didn't have to help me with the kitchen. James sat at the kitchen table and watched me clean up.

"James, in the time you were gone, I saw Chris a lot."

His smile faded when I said that, but he remained silent.

"He really cares about me. He says that . . . that he loves me. And we had sex."

He seemed to have a hard time processing this. He closed his eyes tightly and refused to open them. When he finally did, they were filled with such dread.

"I didn't come here with the hope that things could be any different than they were when I left. I was certain that there was not a possibility at all that you could be with me, because you were pregnant with another man's baby. But now that I come back and you tell me it was a hoax . . . Baby, why would you sleep with him when I know how you feel about me?"

"Stop being so arrogant, James, and keep thinking that I'm not over you."

"You're not over me, Allure. You shared your body with that man, but not your heart. You love me. I know you still love me! Stop fucking with that nigga. Just let me come back home, where I have always belonged."

I shoved him. "Stop trying to confuse me! You're selfish, just like Greg. You screwed up with me, and you don't want me to have a chance to be happy with someone else. I hate you for that shit. If I was by myself, you wouldn't care. Now that I've found someone who wants me, you want to come around and fuck things up for me. And I'm sure that if I take you back, you will cheat on me again. Leave us again." I started swinging at him, throwing punches at his head, at whatever I could come in contact with.

He grabbed my hands in his, and I cried weakly. James started kissing me. And I fought him at first. Then, like a weak bitch, I gave in and we were tonguing it up in my kitchen. He gripped my waist with his hands and explored every crevice of my mouth with his tongue. I did the same to his, until our tongues met and we rubbed them against each other. He forced me to get on my knees, and he raised up my dress, pulled down my underwear. I stopped him.

"You have on no condom, and what if Sierra comes in?"

He stood, pulled me up, and shoved me toward my bedroom. I knew I should stop him, but I didn't.

He dragged me to the bed, even as I cried out in confusion and told him no. He ignored my protests, laid me down, parted my legs, and slipped between them.

"I have not been able to fuck another woman, because all I see is Allure. I couldn't get you out of my fucking head. That's on the life of both my kids."

"No, James, don't." But I protested only with my mouth, not with my body. I welcomed him into me. But when he positioned himself at my vagina, all I saw was Chris. And whether I loved James or not, I could not have sex with him until I straightened things out.

"No!" I shoved him away and started crying. James just sat on the bed with his back to me. It was the first time I had ever rejected his touch. This shit was confusing the hell out of me. I lay on the bed, crying tears of perplexity.

Chapter 18

The next morning I made Sierra and myself a breakfast of pancakes, bacon, and eggs. I knew I had no business doing what I had done last night, and I was consumed with so much guilt that when Chris called and asked to come over, I told him I wasn't feeling good and I would call him on Saturday. Well, now it was Saturday and I couldn't bring myself to do it. I had almost cheated on him. A great guy. The guy of my dreams. It was so fucked up. Here all I said was that I wanted a good man. A man to love me in spite of my flaws, insecurities and fears. A man who was independent and didn't want to live off of me. A man who would love and accept my child. He was all of this and more. And I had almost managed to fuck things up between him and me. I felt like a piece of shit, an utter piece of shit. For whom? James. A man who had always hurt me. What the fuck was I going to do?

"Eat, Mom, before it gets cold. Chris told me that I needed to make sure you ate."

"Okay." But the mention of his name had me choked up. I tried my best not to break down and cry at that table.

The doorbell rang. I stood, turned my back on Sierra, and allowed the tears to fall. Then I quickly wiped them away. I headed to the front door and looked through my peephole. It was Kendra. I forced a smile and opened the door quickly.

"Hey!"

"Hello, Allure."

I moved back so she could step inside.

Sierra ran into the living room. "Hi, Kendra."

"Hey, baby." She kissed Sierra on her cheek and hugged her. Sierra went back into the kitchen to finish her food.

Kendra sat down on one of my couches. I sat across from her.

"So what's up?" I asked.

"What are your birthday plans?"

"Chris said he wants to take me out to dinner to celebrate. You know I been wanting to go to Fleming's. And he is going to take Sierra and me."

She pierced me with a glare. "Right. That is what I wanted to talk to you about."

"Okay."

"Honestly, I don't know. I just feel that you have been a little distant from me. I mean, it's weird, Allure."

I took a deep breath. "I have been dealing with a lot of stuff lately, and I couldn't talk to you—"

"But you're my best friend. I don't ever recall you feeling like you couldn't come to me."

"Let's just say I've made a couple mistakes, and I wasn't comfortable discussing them with you, Kendra."

"Why?"

Kendra was right. I had never, ever kept anything from her. But she was a married woman. And I didn't want her to think less of me. Still, I now wanted to confess to her, get it out the way, so it didn't further affect our friendship. For Kendra to just pop up like that, it must have been bothering her.

"Sierra," I called. "Go take your food into your room and eat."

"Okay."

I waited until I was sure Sierra was completely out of earshot before I continued. "I slept with James while he was still married. It was the night of my sister's funeral.

He has been coming around for Sierra. In all actuality, despite the fact that he was married, I still loved him, and I still love him. I was ashamed to tell you the truth, you being a married woman and all. I honestly didn't think you'd think like a friend. Because you are married, I figured you would think like a married woman."

She tried her best to keep the judgment off her face, but she couldn't. Before she spoke, she inhaled and exhaled. "Allure, I do not respect the fact that you slept with a married man. But regardless, you are my friend and I love you. More important than me judging you for committing adultery, I am concerned with you even dealing with James again, because what I believe is that he will hurt you again."

I knew she would say that. I understood her concern. James had caused Sierra and me a great deal of pain.

"And what about Chris?" Kendra asked.

"I mean, Chris is cool."

"*Cool?* Allure, the man helped you through breast cancer. He was there for you through chemo and radiation! *He* was there, not James."

"James didn't know."

"Are you making excuses for him?"

"No!"

"Well, the point is, Chris is in love with you. Why on earth would you want to jeopardize a good man's love for a low-down, lying ho? You are risking healthy, wholesome love for a man who has hurt you deeply."

I nodded. What could I say to this? She was right.

"James took you for granted and never, ever treated you right. He abandoned you when he got you pregnant. He cheated on you while you were pregnant. Damn near raped you. He left you and your baby when you needed him the most. He came back, fucked you, and married another woman. He probably didn't even wash his dick off. I never thought you would heal from that, because I didn't think *I* could heal from that. But you did. You made it through. Do you really want to revisit that pain again?"

I nodded, silent. I had never seen my friend so furious with me. She was always the calm one.

"Allure, I'm not trying to be a bitch to you, nor am I trying to make you feel worse. I love you and want the best for my friend. Right now you have the absolute world at your feet. A career, a home. Sierra is happy. You have a second chance at living. And you have a man who simply adores you. Don't blow it on James."

"But what if he really has changed, Kendra? He filed for divorce. He said he wants to marry me."

"Allure, please don't do this to yourself." She sounded frustrated. She stood to her feet. "Matter of fact, I don't want to hear any more." She grabbed her purse and walked out.

I didn't stop her, because I didn't know what to say. She was right about all that she had said. But it was not like I had planned for things to go the way that they had gone. And I was confused as hell about how to deal with it. I went into the kitchen and dumped my plate of food in the trash. I now had no appetite for any damn thing.

Chapter 19

The night of my birthday, I was dressed in my best. So was Sierra. She had never wanted to wear dresses, but tonight she wore a pretty sky-blue and white dress for me because it was my day, and she even wore her hair down. I wore a pretty pink dress that Chris had bought for me. It had long sleeves and was tight fitting and backless. I loved how I looked in it, because I was slowly but surely gaining my weight back, so I had a little curve on my hips and butt. I wore a pair of strappy black heels, and I even went out and bought a new wig. This one had Chinese bangs and dark brown highlights. I looked like a million bucks on the outside. But on the inside I was so, so conflicted. And I was consumed with nothing but guilt for what I had done to Chris.

As we backed out of my driveway in Chris's Denali and drove down the street, I noticed he was acting kind of strange. A feeling of alarm hit me. What if he could feel my energy and knew what I had done? He was familiar with James. I had told him that James came around for Sierra after her father got arrested, filling the role of a godfather, and that years ago we had had a relationship that didn't work. I wouldn't say Chris liked it, but he seemed to accept it begrudgingly.

"You okay, baby?" he asked me.

"Yes, I'm fine. Why?"

"Just asking. You don't seem like your normal self."

"I'm okay. Just happy to be okay for my b-day. And I can't believe I'm so old."

"You are still a young tenda," he said, winking at me.

"No, Mommy, you are old," Sierra said.

"Oh, shut up," I joked.

Chris laughed.

When we got to the restaurant, Chris had already made reservations, so we didn't have to wait long.

Once we had settled at our table and had looked at the menu, Chris said, "Order whatever you want, birthday girl."

"Oh, I am," I said with a big smile.

I ended up ordering filet mignon, two lobster tails, and Chipotle Cheddar Macaroni and Cheese. Sierra order crab legs and mashed potatoes. Chris ordered crab legs as well and Fleming's Potatoes. The food was really good, and although I tried to keep a smile on my face, I still felt horrible. Chris was so good to Sierra, and I could have possibly sabotaged that by almost sleeping with James.

After dinner we drove back to my house. When we got to the corner of my street, Chris said, "We have another surprise for you, Allure."

"Really?"

"Yep," Sierra said. "Mom, don't move." She put a blindfold over my eyes and tied it.

I laughed. "What is going on?" I asked.

"You'll see," Sierra told me.

Within a few seconds I felt the car come to a stop. I could hear two car doors opening and closing. Then Chris was over on my side, helping me out of the car.

"Come on, baby." He guided me out of the car and helped me walk. He then helped me up the steps.

"Man, what is going on?" I asked.

"Mommy, you'll see," Sierra said.

When the door to our house opened, Chris pulled the blindfold off of me and I heard, "Surprise!" I saw my mother, Creole, Kendra, her husband, Creole, and

even some of Chris's friends and his cousin. A couple of
Sierra's friends were there as well.

I tossed my head back and laughed. Then I turned and
punched Chris in his arm. He pulled me into his arms,
and he kissed me on my mouth deeply. I heard "Awww"
from a couple people there. Creole, Kendra and Chris's
friends and his cousin all took turns giving me a hug.

There was music playing, and little snacks sat out on the
table, like fruit for dipping in a fondue bowl of chocolate,
various cheeses, pepperoni, and olives. I walked farther
down the table and saw a beautiful cake that resembled
the doll Strawberry Shortcake. There were even several
wrapped gifts for me. I truly felt so special.

"Whose idea was the cake?" I asked.

"Chris's, of course," Katrina said.

As a little girl, I had always loved the Strawberry
Shortcake doll. I remembered telling Chris this. He really
did listen to me.

"Thank you, guys, for this. I feel so special."

"You *are* special," Kendra said.

I smiled at her. I was glad she was no longer angry with
me.

"Open up your gifts. I want to see what you got," Creole
said.

"Okay. Let me run to the bathroom first."

When I got there, I locked the door, sat on the toilet,
and pulled my cell out of my purse. I texted Creole, telling
her to meet me in the bathroom.

A couple minutes later she knocked. I stood, unlocked
the bathroom door, and opened it.

"Bitch, what?" she said.

I yanked her into the bathroom and closed the door
and locked it again. I sat back on the toilet, and she sat on
the edge of the tub.

"I almost slept with James!"

Her eyes got wide. "What?"

"Yes." I started crying. "Creole, I'm so confused. Chris is in love with me, and I don't know if I feel the same, because I feel that I still love James. And he divorced his wife."

"He did?"

"Yes."

"Allure, this is a tough one."

"James says he wants us to get back together. Chris says—"

"What do *you* want?"

"That's the thing. I don't know!" More tears slid down my face.

"Don't cry," she said. She rubbed my back.

"And Kendra was so pissed at me the other day. I told her I had slept with James after my sister's funeral."

"I'm sure she has made her share of mistakes as well."

"Yeah. But I fucked up in so, so many ways. I wish my sister was here, Creole. She would know what to do. I feel so lost without her." I started bawling like a punk. I truly did feel lost. My sister had always given me the direction I needed.

"I know, Allure. But you are going to have to make this choice. And you have to make the right one."

"But who would you pick?"

"I can't answer that for you. I can only say you should choose who you deeply, wholeheartedly love. The one you know you will always love."

I closed my eyes briefly. At times I felt I loved Chris, and at times I felt it was just appreciation for him sticking by me during my chemo. But all the time, I *knew* I loved James. I had never stopped loving James.

"Well, we have to get back outside to your party." She grabbed me by my arm. "Come on, girl. Wipe those tears and come on and enjoy your party. And tonight, when you are alone, you pray on this."

"Okay." I checked myself out in the mirror. I looked fine. So I followed Creole out of the bathroom.

As we walked back to the living room, Creole said, "Enjoy the rest of your night and don't worry about that for now, okay?"

"Okay." I put a smile on my face, and we both walked into the living room.

But when we got there, Creole and I were surprised as hell to see James standing in my living room, next to Sierra. He looked my way and smiled. I smiled back. But I truly felt sick inside about him and Chris being in the same room after what James and I had done the other day.

My mother was shooting James dirty looks from the couch. "Allure, did you?" she whispered.

"No. I knew nothing about this. You know Sierra probably did it."

"Allure!" Kendra beckoned me with her hand over to the couch. "We want to see you open all your gifts." She didn't even mention James being there, so I didn't. She was probably just trying to hold the party together

I sat on the couch, and she put a pretty wrapped gift in my hand. "That is from the hubby and me."

I laughed and started tearing off the wrapping paper. It was a new laptop. I had been needing a new one. I hugged Kendra and then Elijah. "Thanks, you guys."

There were so many gifts there to unwrap, ranging from a Kindle, the newest iPod Touch, a flat-screen TV for my bedroom to various gift cards, from Lakeshore, Barnes & Noble, which I could use for work, and IHOP. I was a die-hard pancake lover. I also received a new pair of UGGs. But with every gift placed on my lap, I kept casting looks Chris's and James's way. But they both seemed to be focused on me opening the gifts rather than on each other.

"Wow. You guys, thank you all for the gifts."

"You are very welcome, missy. You deserve all of this and more." That was Katrina.

"Yes, you do," one of Chris's friends said.

I blushed.

James stared at me from across the room like he wanted to tell me something, but he held back.

I looked away and said, "So I guess it is time to cut the pretty cake."

"Don't you want my gift, baby?" Chris asked.

I chuckled. "I sure do." There were chuckles in the room.

James then honed in on Chris. His face remained neutral, though. No sign of jealousy.

And I'd be damned if Chris didn't get down on his knees!

My hand covered my mouth, and my heart sped up.

Kendra and my mother shrieked.

Chris pulled a velvet box out of his pocket, popped it open, and a beautiful, shiny ring was all up in my face. "Baby, I told you from day one what I wanted, and that's you. All this time I have been spending with you has reaffirmed this. I love you. And I want to marry you, take care of you and Sierra. Give you the best days, years, you could ever imagine." He bit his bottom lip and added, "And some babies. So, Allure Jones, will you marry me?"

Seriously, was I in the twilight zone? This was a moment I had been waiting for, for so long. Here was a good, good man who loved me in spite of my imperfections, in spite of my insecurities, despite my mistakes. A man who worshipped the ground that I walked on. Someone to love me and my daughter. And that man was in front of me, trying to put a ring on it. And yet I was still unsure if I loved him. And I felt torn between him and James. Damn! Why couldn't shit ever go right in my life! Smooth? But I could not tell this man this in front of everyone. So I gave in to the engagement, not really sure if I should say yes . . . or no.

"Yes!"

He smiled and slipped the ring on my finger. Then he kissed my lips. He lifted me from the couch and spun me around. I heard people clapping and cheering for us. It was then that I remembered that James was in the room.

I watched James walk out the front door. Kendra saw it too, but she pretended she didn't.

"I'm going to put on some music," she said.

Creole followed after her. "Here. You can use my iPod. I got all the 'back that ass up' music on there."

Kendra tossed her head back and laughed. "Creole, you are so crazy."

My phone buzzed. It was a text from James.

It read, Meet me outside.

I deleted the text just as my mother and Sierra came over to me and gave me hugs. "Congratulations, Allure."

"Thanks, Mom." I hugged her back and then Sierra. my mother then hugged Chris. Chris then hugged Sierra.

Two of Chris's friends both gave me hugs before pulling him away. It was the perfect distraction.

I told Sierra and my mom, "I'll be right back, you guys."

James was standing on my porch steps with his back to me. When he heard the door open, he waited a few seconds and then, without turning around, asked, "Are you going to marry him, Allure?"

"I really don't know."

He turned around and studied me. "What do you mean, you don't know? If you don't know, why did you take the man's ring?"

"What was I supposed to say, James? That man was there for me during my darkest time. Not you!"

"First off, let's be clear, baby. You don't owe him shit, and you don't owe me shit. You don't make a decision based on what you feel you *owe*. And for the record, yes, he chose to be there. And you took that away from me. *I* would have been there."

"No, you took it away when you made the choices you made over three years ago. You put all this into place, James. All of this is because of you."

"Allure, I'm trying to fix this. I divorced my wife. Does she come around anymore? No. I want to marry you. I'll marry you right fucking now if you let me."

And I'd be damned if this man did not pull a small velvet box out of his pocket and flick it open.

I gasped as he held it out to me. "I came here to propose to you."

"Really? When you knew that Chris would be here, James?"

"Allure, you are what I want. At this point I would move fucking planets to have you, and I'm not worried about another nigga. He doesn't have the history you and I have."

God, James was so damn arrogant. "Please put that away."

"Don't you at least want me to put it on you? It's four carats, baby. I tried to get something you would like. Something you deserved."

I glanced at it. It was beautiful, and so was Chris's ring. But I knew the appearance of both rings wasn't important at the moment.

"I don't care how many carats it is. Just please put it away."

He closed the little box and put it back in his pocket.

"What do you want me to do, James? Why are you putting me through this?" I started crying.

"Baby, I'm not trying to. But you are going to have to decide who you want. You can't marry two men. You need to choose. Is it going to be me or him, Allure?"

I closed my eyes, frustrated, and cried out, "I don't know! Sometimes I feel like I—"

"You what, Allure?" he said, pressing.

Like I love you both. But I couldn't say it out loud.

"Well, I can't stay in there and watch him kiss you and put his hands all over you. When you make a decision about who you want, baby, call me and I'll come back home, where I belong. And this time nothing will ever pull me away from you again. I swear."

I sobbed on my steps. This shit was just too damn hard. James had just made the situation a whole lot worse.

He turned and walked away.

Before I went back inside to the party, I wiped my tears away and put on a smile.

"Allure!" Kendra called, rushing up to me and grabbing one of my hands once I was back in the living room. "Let's blow out your candles."

I joined everyone in the kitchen. Chris held his arms out to me, and I stepped into them as everyone sang "Happy Birthday" to me. They did it Martin Luther King style.

I then blew out my thirty candles. Everyone cheered once I had blown them all out, and Chris kissed me on my lips and whispered, "Happy birthday, baby."

He is so sweet, I thought.

"Smile, baby," he said.

How could I not smile for him? So I did, because he was just so, so sweet to me. So for him, I blocked all the bad thoughts, had a drink, and enjoyed the rest of my birthday.

Chapter 20

I allowed Chris to spend the night, but I told him I was feeling a little weak. He didn't trip and let me to slide on the sex and held me. I knew he wanted some, because his penis continued to poke me in my ass all night long. But he respected my wishes. I had a hard time falling asleep that night because I was going to have to give Chris the ring back until I made a decision. My stomach was literal twisted into knots all night as he held me.

Before he headed out for work the next morning, I laughed at him, because every time he said he was going to leave, he would hesitate and stay longer. Five minutes turned into twenty, and then it got to the point where he was running an hour late.

He gave me one last kiss and was nearly out the door, but then I took a deep breath and said, "I know you have to go, but wait."

"What is it, baby?"

I started crying, and I tugged at his sleeve. "Chris, I appreciate everything that you have done for me, the way you love me and Sierra. But I have to be honest. I'm not one hundred percent sure about marrying you."

"Why not?" He looked hella disappointed.

"There is just some unfinished—"

"Another guy?" he asked evenly.

I didn't answer.

He shook his head. "I know you been hurt before, but, Allure, if you say I've been good to you, then I deserve for you to be good to me. Is it James? I know you said he comes around some times for Sierra, and I trust you, baby. So I never felt the need to question you. . . . But is it him?"

"Yes and no." How could I tell him that I loved him and James? I couldn't. But at the same time I couldn't keep his ring if I was unsure. As a woman, I had to do the right thing.

He closed his eyes and made an exasperated sound. "Are you still sleeping with him?"

"No! Just give me a little time, Chris, to figure some things out." I slid off the ring and handed it back to him.

When I slipped it into his hand, he looked crushed. "Seems like you are pretty much telling me this is over, Allure. After everything. After I told you how I felt about you. Man, and that shit hurts." He turned his back on me, shook his head, then paused for a few seconds before walking away.

"Chris!"

He stopped walking and turned around to face me.

"I know by giving you that ring back, I am taking a chance of losing you." I swallowed. "But all I ask is that you don't completely give up on me. "Please," I begged.

He looked away.

It made me cry all the harder. I turned away.

"Allure."

I wiped my tears and turned back around to face him.

"If you don't want me to give up on you . . ." He grabbed my left hand and slid the ring back on my finger. "While you decide what you want to do, keep this on your finger."

I smiled and hugged him. "I will."

He smiled back and walked to his truck. I watched him drive away. I was relieved that Chris was going to give me the time to figure this shit out and did not completely wash his hands of me. But if he had, I couldn't blame him. However, I couldn't just promise myself to that man until I was sure it was the right choice.

Instead of going to church that Sunday, I dropped Sierra off at my mother's house and drove to the cemetery where my sister was buried. I made my way slowly to her grave site. Looking at it brought back all the memories of that day we laid her to rest and my struggles with it. Being there, I felt like I had lost her all over again even, though it had almost been a year since her death. I struggled going back to my sister's grave because it never felt good. I always left feeling empty inside.and even angry that it had to be my sister who dies. I laid some pretty sunflowers on her grave site. They were her favorite type of flowers. She had always said that they reminded her of a bright day, and that no matter how down she was, they always seemed to make her feel better.

No one was around, so I started talking to her. "I hope I don't look crazy doing this, but hell, if I do, oh well. Damn, Crystal, when I say I miss your ass, it's a straight understatement. I feel like a piece of my heart is missing with you being gone. I'm not trying to be corny, big sis. But you know how they say a person can die, but their spirit can always live on? I hope so. So here I go."

I took a deep breath. "You always been the person in my world who had the final say over Mom, Creole, and Kendra. So I'm going to need you to give me some type of sign, girl. Okay. So James came back around, and you know I never really got over his ass. I have loved him for so long. But then there's Chris, the absolute man of my dreams. He took care of me while I went through chemo, for God's sake. He made love to me with only one titty! He treats me and Sierra like princesses, Crystal. It has been damn near a year, and he has done absolutely nothing at all to hurt me.

"And both of them proposed to me. Well, James sort of. But still, I honestly don't know which one to choose. James hurt me a lot. Chris has never hurt me. I went through so much so many nights, crying over what James did to me. I wasn't really able to move on after our breakup. And I was really out of hope that I would ever land a good man. But Chris restored that hope. Yet I still feel like my heart is pulling me back to James. So that is why I need you to give me some type of intervention, big sister. Send a sign my way, because Lord knows, I need to make a decision. Even if you throw some dirt in my eyes or trip me, it's okay. Shit, do something to help me decide what to do. Because one way or another, I have to decide."

I started crying again. "Damn! I said I wasn't going to do this shit. But why did God have to take you? I know I shouldn't question His will, but damn, Crystal. I needed you here on this earth. I know that is selfish to say." I couldn't say anything else, because I started sobbing and dropped to my knees. I broke out bawling like a baby, like I was back there the day that we buried her. I wiped my eyes and my snotty nose with my forearm. "Like I was saying, Crystal, please give me a sign. I need your guidance. I love you." I kissed her tombstone, rose, and walked back to my car.

Chapter 21

Before I got on the freeway, I called my mother and told her I was on the way to pick up Sierra.

"Well, we are not home right now. We're at IKEA, doing a little shopping. I'll drop her off to you when we are done."

"Okay, Mom."

I set out for home instead. I was glad I would be alone, because it would give me the time to think.

When I unlocked the front door and stepped inside my house, flicking on the lights, I was scared out of my mind to see three figures sitting on my living room couch. James's wife and his two kids. It wasn't just that, that had me shaken up. The bitch was aiming a gun at me.

"Next time make sure Sierra's windows are all locked in this piece of shit of a house. Mine is three times bigger. You think you did something because you bought this closet? I wish the president would get rid of these home-buyer programs. Makes ghetto, low-budget bitches like you think you are on my level."

"What the fuck are you doing in my house?"

She ignored my question and said calmly, "Have a seat."

When I hesitated, she pulled the safety on her gun. I sat down on the couch across from her.

"Boys, this is Allure. She is the bitch that your father has been fucking. The one he appears to love, divorced me for, and broke up our happy home for. Say hi."

"Hi," they both chorused. Their eyes were wide with fear. This was a nutty woman.

I shook my head at this crazy bitch.

"Say hi to my children!" she yelled.

"Hi, boys," I said.

"Now, you seemed to have thought your problems with me were over, didn't you, Allure? That I was just going to lie down and let you take my husband from me, huh?"

"I—"

"Shut up! I let you do a lot of talking last time. Today I'm going to talk and you are going to shut the fuck up! In fact . . ." She stood and walked over to me with the gun pointed. With her free hand, she slapped the shit out of me.

The side of my face stung. I wanted to punch that bitch.

"You interrupt me again, and I'm going to punch the shit out of you. You got it?" She shoved my head back.

"Yeah. I got it."

"When I met James, you were knocked up. But as I have said before, I didn't care. I felt I deserved him. So I did everything in my power to get him. Good sex, good food, stimulating conversation, and the promise that I could make him happier than you made him. He loved me at first. When he left you for good, I was like, 'Yes! I finally have him.' But I know how men are. I represented something new, refreshing. Then I got old to him, and he wanted to go back to you. I figured if got knocked up he'd stick around. So I poked holes in the condoms. I knew he was scared to buy them, because he never wanted his precious Allure to find out he was cheating. Then, finally, I got pregnant. And I'm sure you don't know where yours is, but *my* father put the pressure on him to do the right thing and marry me. And he proposed. Yet, bitch, you were still in his heart, no matter what I did. Miss Allure, you have positively ruined my life. You're nothing but a used-up battered woman!"

She took the gun and whacked me in the mouth with it. Her blow drew blood. Blood streamed down my face.

"Are you surprised that I know about your past? You used to be on welfare, for God's sake. You ain't shit. And you had the audacity to break up my marriage?"

She used her free fist to pummel me in my face. I dropped my head in my lap to stop her assault.

She started breathing hard and stepped back. "Now, let's get down to business. Boys, take your spots, like I explained to you." The boys obediently went into my kitchen.

"Get up, bitch." She kicked me, and I stood to my feet. She pressed the gun into my back. "Walk!"

I walked into my kitchen. When I got there, there were four glasses on the table.

"In case you are wondering why there are four glasses on the table, let me explain," she growled. "Each glass has cyanide in it. James hurt me. He broke up my home, and I'm not going to lie down and take it. I'm going to take the three things James loves the most, his sons and, bitch, you. Then, since I will have pretty much lost everything that means anything to me, I figure I might as well join you guys."

This bitch was crazy. She was really going to kill her kids over a man? I was hurt when James left me, but I could never hurt Sierra because of it.

"You can't be serious," I said.

"Bitch!" She punched me again. "I told you not to talk!"

"Children, pick up those glasses, like I instructed you earlier."

"Yes, Mommy," the older one said. I knew he was Ryder from the pics that James had shown me.

The younger, who, I remembered, James had said was JJ, chimed in after his brother. "'Kay, Mommy."

She aimed the gun at me. "And, you, grab that glass."

I watched, horrified, as the boys did as they had been instructed and each picked up a glass. Damn, I hoped my mother and Sierra got here soon. It was times like this when I wished James would pop up.

"Grab it, Allure!"

I did, and I turned to look at the two boys. They both hesitated as they held the glasses in their hands.

"Now, put the glass to your lips," Latasha ordered.

The older one, Ryder, sniffed the contents of his glass and said, "Mommy, do I have to drink this? It smells really bad."

"Drink it now!"

The older son started crying, and once he started, the younger one started in as well.

Latasha started crying too and said, "Goddamn it! I don't have time for this now! We talked about this already. This is the only way. Daddy doesn't want us anymore. He wants that bitch and her bastard kid."

"I want Daddy," the older one said.

She stepped forward with the gun still in her hand and snatched the younger boy. "You will drink it." She took the glass out of his hand and said, "Open your mouth, JJ!"

While her eyes were on her son, I seized the opportunity and, with lightning speed, splashed her face with the cyanide-laced liquid in my glass.

When the liquid hit her face, she panicked, dropped the gun, released her son, and touch her face with her hands, screaming all the while. I wasted no time in rushing her. I knocked her crazy ass to the floor and started punching the shit out of her.

"You crazy-ass bitch! Why in the fuck would you try to kill your kids over a man?"

She tried to fight back, but she had been temporarily blinded by the cyanide. I continued to hold her down with my legs and punch her in the face. She used all her strength to flip me off of her. I fell on the floor but got up quickly. She stood as well.

Her youngest son now had the gun in his hand.

"JJ, give me the gun!" she said.

"No! Don't give it to her please!" I begged. "I'm going to get you guys away from this crazy bitch!"

"JJ, this is Mommy talking to you, baby. Mommy loves you so much. Please give me the gun."

Poor baby looked too conflicted.

When he rushed up to her and attempted to place the gun in her hand, I figured my only chance at living was to try to get out of that house, so I took off running toward the front door. But it was too late. The bitch started firing at me, and bullets were flying everywhere around me. I ducked and managed to get the door open, and I ran through it. Once outside, I screamed for my life as I ran down my steps.

"Help!" I yelled. Latasha was on my heels, still firing shots. I had made it halfway out of my yard when a shot finally hit me in my back, dropping me to my knees in the grass.

The pain was unimaginable. She kicked me in my back, smiled, and aimed the gun at my face. Her boys ran right past me and out of my yard. She ignored them. Thank God they wouldn't be hurt on account of her. I looked down at my chest as blood oozed from me. Shit was hurting like crazy. I winced and looked up at her.

She cocked back the safety, but before she could fire again, I heard a siren. I looked behind me and saw a squad car speeding down my street at high speed.

Latasha took off running toward my house. She rushed up the steps, ran inside, and closed the door.

Seconds later, a cop kneeled down next to me. "Were you shot?"

"Yes, and those little boys running away are the kids of the woman who just shot me. Be careful!" I warned. "That bitch is crazy."

He pulled his radio off his belt and requested backup. "We need backup, and we have one victim down!"

I was growing weaker by the second.

The cop and his partner walked stealthily toward my house with their guns aimed at my front door. They crept up the steps, but before they could open the door, a single shot was fired.

I felt myself getting weaker and weaker, until suddenly I saw whiteness and a hand reaching out to me and heard a familiar voice calling my name.

Chapter 22

Losing my sister in a car accident, check. Having breast cancer, check. Getting shot in the back by my ex's crazy-ass ex-wife . . . priceless.

"Damn, bitch. You got more damn lives than a fucking cat!" Creole exclaimed as she walked into my room at the hospital. This was her third time coming to see me. She sat on the edge of my bed. "Hi, Mom," she told my mother.

My mom was seated across from me. We'd been watching Soap Operas. She chuckled. Sierra was at school, and my mother was going to pick her up when she left the hospital. "Hi, Creole."

I laughed. "Shut up, Creole."

But maybe I did have more lives than your average cat. Because, for sure, my heart had stopped on that lawn and my black ass was crossing over. I knew I had crossed over because I saw my damn sister. I later found out that the paramedics in the ambulance had used a defibrillator to bring me back. I figured no one would believe that I had seen my sister, so I kept it to myself.

I grimaced, as I was trying my best to eat the nasty-ass hospital food. They had said it was turkey soup. Mess tasted like crap.

"Damn, Allure. That is one crazy bitch. I can't stop thinking about it," Creole said.

Three days had passed since that day, and I felt lucky as hell to be alive. One of my neighbors had heard the screaming coming from my house and had called the police. Thank God. As they were in route, they heard the gunshots.

The day of the incident my mother, Sierra, Chris, Kendra, and Creole had rushed to the hospital. I was just lucky to be alive. I had lost so much blood, I couldn't see straight and was going in and out of consciousness. But they had managed to remove the bullet and had stitched me up good. I was completely out that day and didn't remember much. It wasn't until the next day that I was even able to focus or talk. Creole had told me that James came to the hospital at some point, distraught. She said that once the doctor informed him that I was okay, James left the hospital. And after the conversation James and I had had this morning, I was pretty sure that I wouldn't hear from him for a long time. I fought back tears just thinking about it.

I understood. I knew that finding out that his ex-wife had shot the woman he loved and had tried to poison his kids was just too much for James to handle. And then she had turned the gun on herself. I knew the experience had to be a traumatic one for her poor sons. I was so glad that they didn't drink that cyanide.

My gunshot wound wasn't fatal. But Latasha's self-inflicted gunshot wound sure was. The gunshot killed her. But I had heard that most gunshots to the head ended in death. I was glad that she had shot me in the back instead.

In the past three days Kendra had also been to the hospital every day to check on me. Chris, my mother, and Sierra stayed overnight at the hospital all three days, even though I told them I was fine. And although he was always all smiles, I knew the whole situation was bugging Chris . . . and he was waiting for the right time to bring it up to me.

I looked up and smiled as Chris came into the room with bags of In-N-Out.

"Hey, Ms. Creole. Hey, baby." He winked at me.

"What it do, Chris?" Creole asked.

He chuckled. "I got a bunch of Double-Doubles and fries. There is plenty, so you are welcome to it, Creole. Sorry, baby. This is too heavy for you right now."

I groaned. "The struggle."

He, my mother, and Creole laughed as Chris handed them each a burger and a container of fries.

"Good looking, Chris, 'cause I'm starving. But we won't torture you with it, Allure. Come on, Mom. Let's go eat it in the lobby," Creole said.

My mother stood, but before she walked out, she refilled my pitcher of water and sat it on the table next to me.

Once they were both gone, Chris sat on the edge of my bed. "So . . ."

"Look, Chris, I know you are like, 'What the hell is going on?'"

"I know what is going on, baby. Only a fool wouldn't. But did you sleep with James while he was married to her?"

I knew his opinion of me would change once he found out the truth, but I had to be honest with him.

"Yes."

He looked away.

"The night of my sister's funeral, I got drunk and we slept together. But that is the only time, I swear, Chris." I closed my eyes briefly. "James used to be the love of my life. We lived together. We had a child together who died. For a long time, even after he decided to leave me and marry another, I could not fathom loving another man."

"Do you still love him?"

"Yes."

"What?" He looked shocked that I had said it so easily.

"I said yes."

"Then, Allure, I guess you have given me my answer. That is who you choose."

"Ask me if I love you."

He shook his head at me. "It's not possible for—"

"Just ask me!"

He took a deep breath. "Allure, do you love me?"

"Yes! And I know that sounds stupid, but believe me, Chris. The day I got shot, as I was lying in that grass, I passed over. Call me crazy, but I saw my sister. It was like she was alive! She broke it down for me. She said part of me will always love James. I loved what we two were. And loneness convinced me that I still loved him. If I really loved him, I would have never been able to fall for you or give my body to you. I will always *have* love for him, but the person who I wholeheartedly love . . . is you."

He looked up at the last two words, *is you*. He had a huge smile on his face. "So what are you saying, baby?"

"I'm saying that Allure Jones and her drama are officially over. I know what I want, and I know who I am supposed to be with. That person, I can say without a doubt, is you. And since you put a ring on it, I'm marrying you. If you'll still have me, baby."

Amazed, he leaned over and planted kiss after kiss on my lips. He then hugged me a little too tight.

"Owww!" I yelled, giggling.

"Oh, I'm sorry, baby."

"It's okay."

"So are you serious? You are going to marry me?"

"Yes. I do. I do. I do. I do. I do!"

He tossed his head toward the ceiling and busted up laughing.

Epilogue

Two and a half years later . . .

"Finally!" I yelled, excited.

I moved my fat, six-months-pregnant ass alongside my family to our booth at Lucille's at Long Beach Towne Center. I was having a serious craving for some barbecue.

"I'll sit next to Bralynn," Sierra said.

I chuckled as Chris sat our fat-cheeked, one-year-old son, Bralynn, in a high chair next to Sierra. He then sat down next to me and rubbed my stomach. That fool couldn't wait to get me knocked up again, and he hadn't waited long.

I smiled and kissed his lips.

When I pulled away my husband continued to stare at me. "What are you thinking about, baby?" he asked.

"Oh, nothing. Just about how happy I am to be your wife and how I'm going to tear my ribs up!"

I thought back to two and a half years ago. Once I told Chris that I had chosen him, in those two weeks I remained in the hospital, my ass wasted no time and called a wedding planner. And six and a half months later was the big day. Chris and I got married at the Wyndam Hotel in Irvine. I thought back to that day. *I mean it was the wedding of my dreams. We went all out. Pretty much, Christopher said the décor and everything else was purely up to me. I opted for the colors pink and silver. I chose roses and carnations for our flowers.*

Chris, he only wanted to plan the menu and hire the DJ. He definitely went all out with food and drink! Plain and simple we planned to turn up! I mean we were serving a freaking crab boil, fried cat fish, red beans and rice, gumbo, lobster ceviche, filet mignon and loaded potatoes. We weren't playing. My cake was four tiers and each tier was a different flavor. The bottom white with a raspberry filling with white chocolate frosting, the third was a freaking Carmel cake for my boo the next tier was my personal fave, banana cake with cream cheese frosting and the next tier double chololate with chocolate frosting for Sierra. I had a long twenty two inch weave put in my hair. I wore it in nothing but Shirley Temple curls with a part down the middle and a Tiara. Now when it came to my dress selection, it took me forever and ever to decide on the right dress. I was so confused as to which one to choose I drove everybody around me except for Christopher insane. And the one I chose definitely was the right one. It was heart shaped at the top and princess cut with a long trail and covered in such a pretty beading and lace. True to myself, I wore pink strappy heels underneath and to Creole's dismay I even had my toes and nails polished pink. I didn't care it was my wedding my day. Sierra was assigned flower girl and I had no maid of honor. That position was only for my sister, and although she wasn't physically there, she was there in spirit. Kendra, Creole, Katrina and Chris's younger sister were bridesmaids. His sister, parents, aunt, and grandparents flew down and were a part of the festivities as well as both my brothers who gave me away. And although my sister wasn't there, Kendra and Creole kept me so entertained with jokes and champagne that I was in nothing but excitement and bliss.

"Okay it's time for you to open up this shit," Creole said as I sat on my bed in my robe. Dwele's, Old Lovas was playing on my iPod. I had just had my make-up done and my hair.

Kendra laughed at how crass Creole was. The other ladies in the wedding were in their separate room getting ready and would be in mine any second to help me. Sierra and my mother were also present in my room.

Creole had sat on my bed three times. Each one was labeled something different: something blue, something old and something borrowed.

"Now I won't take full credit for this, you mother and Siera helped me also."

I unwrapped the first box labeled something blue. It was a sexy lace garter with the name Christopher inscribed on it.

I screaked. "I love it!"

Creole helped me put it on. "I figured your ass would since the day you decided preparing for the wedding you've been wearing his name on every article of clothing your ass had."

We all laughed. She was right. Ever since I chose Chris I went bananas and found this business that inscribes words on clothes. I went out and got a sweatsuit with the words, "Soon to be Mrs. Wallace" embroided on the back of the top and on the bottom." I had a tank top with "I love Chris" And I had some under wear that said Wifey on them. The other pair said Chris's and another pair with his initials. Thing was, I was so damn happy to have a great man in my life. A man that positivley adored and loved me so I wanted to share it with the word. I mean for so long I waited for this moment and it was here. And he wasn't going anywhere. He had shown me this in so, so many ways that he was here to stay.

The next box she gave me was something labeled borrowed. "Your mother in law supplied this." I opened the box and found a really pretty pearl bracelet."

My mother helped me put it on.

"The next gift is from your mother." I opened the box and pulled out what looked like a hankerchief. But it didn't feel like a hankerchief.

"Its made from one of Sierra's old baby blankets."

"Awww. Thanks mom."

"That was creative," Kendra said. "It's something old and you know you'll need it because something tell me you will be tearing up quite a bit today."

I smiled. The song on my Ipod switched from Dwele to Faith Evans's, "Reasons."

I smiled and closed my eyes as the song played.

"What are you doing weirdo?" Creole asked.

I chuckled. "You don't know how many times I've played this song in the house while cleaning up and in my car on the way to pick up Sierra, going to school or to work and I have cried and cried and wished that God would send me someone. And he just never came. I gave up so many times. And now he's here. The one God sent to me." I shook my head and tried my best not to cry so I wouldn't mess up my make up. "And how he's here."

"Aww Allure. Yes he is." Kendra said. "Now ahhhh. Whats next?" Kendra joked.

We laughed and we all looked up at Creole while she looked around whistling.

"See what had happened was."

"Creole!" Kendra exclaimed. "You were supposed to supply some old, new, borrowed and blue. You left out the new fool."

"Sierra was supposed to"

Sierra cracked up laughing. "No I wasn't."

"Fool don't blame my baby." I joked.

That's when there was a knock on the door.

"Creole went to the door to see who it was.

I looed down at the hankerchief again.

"Look who it is, Christopher, the stalker. You know you ain't supposed to be here right now," Creole said joking.

My mother and I laughed from the bed.

Kendra went up to the door. "Chris, you know you not supposed to be here."

"I just wanted to check on my future wife."

I tiptoed towards the door.

"Allure," my mom said. "Don't let him see you. That's bad luck."

I chuckled. "I won't mom."

I stood on the opposite side of Kendra and Creole on the wall.

As Chris spoke, I slid one of my hands in the slit on the door. I blushed when I felt lips on it.

"Hey hey that's enough. Save that for tonight you two freaks," Creole guided me away.

"Okay well give this to my boo for me please."

"Okay Chris now go away."

I heard the door close and Kendra come over with a Tiffany's bag in her hand.

"Whats all this?" I asked.

"From your future hubby.

"Open them bad boys up!" I exclaimed. "I've never gotten anything from Tiffany's before. My heart started pounding a little faster.

Th first box was really tiny. When Kendra opened the box, I shrieked at the beautiful diamond tear drop earrings inside.

"Wow." My mother said.

The next box was mid-size rectangular shaped. It was a diamond tennis braclet. It was flawless white gold, encircled by diamonds that sparkled against my skin.

"Now you know that has to be at least six carots!" Creole exclaimed. "I know cause I went with him and Ericka to pick out the pieces."

The next box held a necklace dripping with diamonds. I gasped as Kendra laid it against my neck.

Creole yelled, "Your ass is officially spoiled! Allure can you imagine how it is going to be when youre official?"

I smiled as Kendra assisted me in putting everything on.

"You got some stacks on you."

"Mom you look so pretty already."

"Thanks Sierra."

"Shine bright like a diamond," Creole sang.

"Okay," My mother said, "Let's get your dress on so we can get going."

It took the assistance of my mother, Creole, Kendra and even little Sierra to assist me.

As they belted the corset in the back and I struggled to suck my stomach in Creole said, "You know your ass was supposed to lose some poundage."

"Well you know how it is when you're in love you gain that love weight."

"Naw you gained that cream cheese pound cake, fried chicken and macaroni and cheese, weight."

Everyone started laughing.

I was just relieved that it fit. I stared at myself in the full length mirror and in all actuality could not believe this shit! Me? I was getting married? I had found the man of my dreams and he had put a ring on my finger.

Crazy as it sounded, this is not how I imagined things. It was better. I said silently, "When I say thank you God I mean it." Crazy that after all these years I finally have when I never thought I would. I felt so lucky man. So incredibly blessed.

All my bridesmaids joined us in the room. They all exclmied at how pretty I looked. There ws nothing but excited bussel. Ericka was pouring everyone champagne and we all stood around for a toast.

Katrina lead the toast. "Lets toast to love. Allure is the best thing that could have happened to my cousin. You are a reat addition to the family. May you have the best wedding day ever!"

"Cheers!" we all said.

As our glasses clinked together I saw the door to the bridal dressing room open and James strode inside.

Several faces including mine, were in shock, *and Kendra, she was totally disgusted.*

He ignored everyone and stood in front of me. "Hi," he said. "I know I probably shouldn't be here, but I need to just talk to you for, like, three minutes."

I took a deep breath, and I turned to everyone who was in the room, my mother, Sierra, Creole, Kendra, Katrina and Chris's sister "Would you guys excuse us please?"

Everyone walked out, casting looks our way as they went. The only one who objected was Kendra. "Allure," she said sweetly, "Don't forget this is your wedding day."

"I know. Just go, Kendra."

"All right." She walked out of the room.

His eyes raked up and down my body. "You look really beautiful."

*I thought back to the last time I had spoken to him,
when I told him I had made my choice. He had gotten
so angry and had yelled at me. "Allure, with what I'm
going through, you tell me that shit now?" he'd said.
"That you chose him over me? No, you don't love that
man. You love me. I know you do. Why are you doing
this to me, baby?"*

*I was crying hysterically on the other end of the phone,
because the hardest thing I had to do was tell James
that I was not going to marry him. I knew a part of me
would always love James, but I loved Chris very much. I
couldn't see that before, because I'd been so wrapped up
in the past and the idea of James being that missing piece
from the puzzle. I had felt that piece had to be him. But it
wasn't. If James and I had ever been meant to be, things
wouldn't have been so complicated for us. With James,
I had experienced too much heartache for things ever to
be considered healthy. I knew that he had tried to do the
right thing by divorcing his wife, but really it was too late.
And we just weren't meant to be. When I focused on the
hard facts, I realized that my heart had spoken, and it had
spoken Chris's name, not James's. The spirit of my sister
had confirmed it for me.*

*"You know what? I hate you, Allure. After all I did,
you don't want me? I left my wife. Now she is dead. My
kids don't have a mother! You are the reason for all of
this! Fuck you, Allure!"*

*I ended the called and sobbed on my bed. The pain
I felt in my heart was so intense, I called my nurse,
pretended my gunshot wound was bothering me so they
would give me some more pain medication that would
put me to sleep. They did, and sleep was what I used to
escape his words and the overall situation.*

*James's words now, in the dressing room, snapped
me out of my thoughts. "You look beautiful. The way I
had always imagined you would look."*

"Thank you."

"Listen. I know the last time we talked, I said some things that I shouldn't have said, and I put all the blame for what happened on you." He swallowed. *"But I know it is not your fault."* He cleared his throat, and his lips started trembling. A cluster of tears slid down his cheeks. *"God, this is hard."*

My eyes started to water.

"Allure." He wiped his tears away. *"I want you to know that despite everything that has happened, I am really, really happy for you, baby. I fucked up, and I lost you. Sometimes I think that even if you had chosen me, I would never have had the old Allure. Maybe it's because of all the wrong I had done, but . . . you didn't look at me the same way. There was always anger and mistrust in your eyes. Even in good moments. I don't blame you, because what I did to you could scar a woman forever. And him . . . when you looked at him, it was the way you used to look at me. You loved him then and didn't even realize it, baby."*

A sob escaped him. *"I saw it that night at your birth-day party. I knew I had lost then. But my pride wouldn't let me admit it and move on. I still wanted to fight for something I knew deep down couldn't be, something I no longer deserved. Had I done things the right way years ago and not been so selfish, you would be married to me. And as for my wife, she started taking antidepressant pills not long after JJ was born. She had postpartum depression. I believe that has a lot to do with why she started behaving the way she did. And you're not to blame for what she did. You never were. I'm sorry I blamed you that day. It just is so hard to let you go and move on but this is what I have to do. I just want to say good-bye and wish you nothing but the best, baby."*

He leaned over and kissed me on my lips. And I didn't stop him. He pulled back, stared at me with such a hurtful look on his face that I broke out in sobs. His face crumbled, and he started crying again. Heavy sobs racked his body. He looked like he wanted to come to me, comfort me. But he didn't. Instead, he backed away from me and walked out. And I cried like a baby for a few minutes, and then, like I always did, I dried my tears. But they came back and back and back. I ended up having to get my makeup done over. And though I continued to cry, I realized that James had confirmed that I had made the right choice. So I said a prayer, got many hugs from my bridal party, and was reminded that I was about to marry the man of my dreams. So I put a dazzling smile on my face.

"The Most Beautiful Girl In The World" played as my bridesmaids walked down the aisle.

After Creole, the last person, the music chimed in for me to go.

"You ready?"

I smiled at my older brother Bobby, took a deep breath and intertwined one of my arms in his. He place a kiss on my right cheek and as, "At This Time" by Algebra Blessett played, I walked down the aisle. This is my moment I told myself silently. As I walked I had nothing but tunnel vision and only saw Chris as he stood like he was transfixed by me.

Once I made it to where Chris stood he and my brother shook hands.

Then Chris joined his hand in mine.

"Who gives this woman to this man?" The pastor asked.

"We do," my brother and mother said.

"So we are all here to see the union of two wonderful people."

I looked in Chris's eyes and he winked at me. I don't know why but just that gesture made my heat skip a beat.

"Chris Allure told me that your love and care for her is unreal. Allure, Chris said that ever since he met you, he can't imagine another day without you."

Chris squeezed my hand tighter.

"I have spent a lot of time with this couple since they came to me and requested that I marry them and from what I observed from these too . . . This love that these two people have for each other is the type of love that is so hopeful so is so empowering because it shows that true and wholesome love can still exist. I enjoyed watching them together because there is so much peace there. He is that night and shining armor that Allure has been looking for her whole life. And she shows her appreciation for Chris being this by being the epitome of a real woman. She gives him a love that isn't watered down, and void of conflict. And he returns all of this by being that strong, honest and stable man that Allure and Sierra needs. Plain and simple, Allure compliments Chris and Chris compliments her. There is no one more suited for Allure and no one more suited for Chris.

I felt tears slide down my face at his words.

Chris wiped them away.

"Now this couple wrote their own vows. Allure will go first."

"When I saw that this." I gestured with my hands. "All of this felt like a dream. I cannot believe I'm here. And I'm so elated I'm here with you baby. I have endured so many ups and downs so many drag out battles to be standing here lets just say."

"Amen" I knew that was Creole.

I looked her way and chuckled.

"I have had my heart broken so many times. Every time I thought he was the one, I realized he was merely another

mistake. And all I ever wanted was to have a man to love me and my daughter. So in all actuality I almost gave up. But this man. I don't know how to describe what he has done for me. I feel like God shined on me the day I met Chris. I struggled with writing my vows because when it comes to summing up just ow good this man in front of me is I have a lack of terminology because the best words in the world are understaments to just how good he is. But I can say that with him my blessing seem infinite. And each day waking up and knowing I have him in my life makes each day feel like Christmas. And I have him, ya'll he's mine!" I hit my chest in emphasis.

"You got me baby," he said.

People started laughing.

"Chris, just know baby that, I strive try to be all you require. Maybe even more. I vow never to restructure you, but accept you as you are, as you have taken me. And Understand that because I have you The world itself seems to be mine. I love you baby."

Chris leaned over and kissed me.

"Hold on there. Kissing is last You two not officially married yet."

There was more laughter.

"Now Chris," The pastor said. "You may now read your vows.

"Let me just say that I have never in my life met a woman like Allure. And I want to take this moment now as I read my vows to show Allure how great of a woman she is. Ya'll listen up. She is seriously the best woman I have ever had. And what is so insane about this woman is the fact that she doesn't even see how phenomenal she is. Thing was, I saw it from day one within the first five minutes of meeting her and I told myself I'm about to

snatch her up before another man sees how much of a gold mine she is and steals the opportunity away from me. When I look at her I see beauty, cause my baby is fine. But I also I see an angel. My baby is so lovely."

"Awwwe," was chorused. *I looked over at Creole and Kendra, and Creole were crying as well and fanning her face at Chris's words.*

"I mean damn!" *Chris said twirling me around.*

More laughter

"What makes her shine is the fact that she is a caring soul. When I come to her, after I've had a long day, it doesn't matter what she is doing. She turns those brown eyes on me and in that moment treats me like I'm the most important person in her world. I've see her do that for friends, family, and her students. And her words are always one hundred percent genuine. She will sacrifice all her time for those around her until all her energy is zapped. She carries so much respect for me, almost honoring me as her man. Well I'm here today to tell you how honored I feel to have gotten this far that you have chosen me baby. I don't take the job of being your husband lightly. I will be there for you and Sierra every day of the rest of our lives. Will be a provider, father, friend and confidant. I'm privileged to do all of this. I'm lucky as hell to have a woman like you. For me you exceed perfection and like I said when I proposed to you. I'm here to give you the best days, years you could ever imagine. I'm going to love you with no limits. I already do, I'm going to treasure you baby this is nothing compared to how happy and great life will be. I love you Allure Jones. At this point I was sobbing at his words. I knew my makeup was ruined and there was snot running down my face but I didn't care because this moment was absolutely priceless.

"We need the rings," the Pastor said.

Once Kendra passed me Chris's and Chris's best friend passed him mine, the pastor said as we slid them on each others fingers. "Repeat after me. "With this ring I thee wed.

I stared into Chris's eyes as we both repeated the statement.

"By the-"

"Hold on there pastor," Chris said. "Sierra get on up here baby girl."

Sierra came and stood in front of us. Chris pulled something out of his pocket. " It was a tiny diamond ring. He slid it onto Sierra's second finger. "My promise is also to you. To be the best father I can be to you." He leaned in and kissed her on her right cheek. She blushed.

When she stepped down, the pastor cleared his throat and said. "I, through the grace of God am extremely proud to introduce you all to Mr. and Mrs. Christopher Wallace. You may kiss your bride."

And Chris did in fact he lifted me off my feet for the kiss and I didn't mind one bit.

"Did you hear me babe?" Chris said sapping me out of my thoughts.

"Huh?"

"I asked if you wanted the usual appetizer?"

"Yep."

There were times when I thought about James. I mean, we had some good times, and there were times when he was good to me. He was the father of my first son. That couldn't be erased, nor did I want it to be. I thought there would always be just a tiny piece of my heart reserved for James. From time to time he would reach out to Sierra, send her Christmas and birthday gifts. He even came to some of her basketball games. But he respected my space, my marriage, and stopped popping up. I always prayed that James would find love and happiness again.

And Lord, when I told you I had the world's best husband, it was an understatement. He fulfilled every need that Sierra, Bralynn, and I had. He was hardworking, loving, kind, patient, and understanding and was such an awesome stepfather and Daddy. He loved Sierra like she was his own. On his way home from work he would always call and ask if I or the kids needed anything. He would come home from work stinky and sweaty and would give me a kiss that felt like what was on his mind and heart was deposited in my mouth. He was a simple man. He wanted a good meal, some quality time, and some loving, and he was happy. At night, when he made love to me, he always left me with chills. He would hold me tight, and I had to wrestle him just to get away to use the bathroom.

He accepted my past and never threw it in my face, what I had been through, my reasons for sometimes feeling insecure. He helped me work through any issues I had. And if they came up again, he never got mad. He would say, "Hey, let's address them again." And he said he would address them again and again if he needed to, until I got the point that he was here to stay and that he loved me unconditionally. He always said he had come to restore, and he did. I had never thought I could trust a man again. But that man . . . I trusted him with all I had. I knew he would protect me on all levels, because he had done so from day one.

Every Friday was date night, every Saturday was family night, and on Sundays we sat in church like a beautiful family. Like the families I would see when it was just Sierra and me, and I wished for the same. Now I had it. Everything I had hoped, cried, and prayed for was in my hands. I couldn't be happier. I also remained 100 percent cancer free.

I let go of the past, and Chris, Sierra, Bralynn, and I, we moved forward like the family I had always dreamed of having.

The End

About the Author

Karen Williams, who also writes as Braya Spice, is the author of *Harlem on Lock, The People Vs. Cashmere, Dirty to the Grave, Thug in Me, Sweet Giselle, The Demise of Alexis Vancamp, Aphrodisiacs: Erotic Short Stories,* and *Dear Drama.* In addition, she contributed to the anthologies *Around the Way Girls 7* and *Even Sinners Have Souls Too.* She graduated from California State University, Dominguez Hills, with a Bachelor's Degree in Literature and Communications. She works as a Probation Officer and lives in Bellflower, California, with her two kids, Adara, sixteen, and Bralynn, four.

Notes

Notes

ORDER FORM
URBAN BOOKS, LLC
97 N18th Street
Wyandanch, NY 11798

Name (please print):_____

Address: _____

City/State: _____

Zip: _____

QTY	TITLES	PRICE
	3:57 A.M Timing Is Everything	$14.95
	A Man's Worth	$14.95
	A Woman's Worth	$14.95
	Abundant Rain	$14.95
	After The Feeling	$14.95
	Amaryllis	$14.95
	An Inconvenient Friend	$14.95
	Battle of Jericho	$14.95
	Be Careful What You Pray For	$14.95
	Beautiful Ugly	$14.95
	Been There Prayed That:	$14.95
	Before Redemption	$14.95

Shipping and handling-add $3.50 for 1st book, then $1.75 for each additional book.

Please send a check payable to:

Urban Books, LLC

Please allow 4-6 weeks for delivery

ORDER FORM
URBAN BOOKS, LLC
97 N18th Street
Wyandanch, NY 11798

Name(please print):_____

Address: _____

City/State: _____

Zip: _____

QTY	TITLES	PRICE
	By the Grace of God	$14.95
	Confessions Of A Preachers Wife	$14.95
	Dance Into Destiny	$14.95
	Deliver Me From My Enemies	$14.95
	Desperate Decisions	$14.95
	Divorcing the Devil	$14.95
	Faith	$14.95
	First Comes Love	$14.95
	Flaws and All	$14.95
	Forgiven	$14.95
	Former Rain	$14.95
	Forsaken	$14.95

Shipping and handling-add $3.50 for 1st book, then $1.75 for each additional book.
Please send a check payable to:
Urban Books, LLC
Please allow 4-6 weeks for delivery

ORDER FORM
URBAN BOOKS, LLC
97 N18th Street
Wyandanch, NY 11798

Name (please print):_____

Address: _____

City/State: _____

Zip: _____

QTY	TITLES	PRICE
	From Sinner To Saint	$14.95
	From The Extreme	$14.95
	God Is In Love With You	$14.95
	God Speaks To Me	$14.95
	Grace And Mercy	$14.95
	Guilty Of Love	$14.95
	Happily Ever Now	$14.95
	Heaven Bound	$14.95
	His Grace His Mercy	$14.95
	His Woman His Wife His Widow	$14.95
	Illusions	$14.95
	In Green Pastures	$14.95

Shipping and handling-add $3.50 for 1st book, then $1.75 for each additional book.

Please send a check payable to:

Urban Books, LLC

Please allow 4-6 weeks for delivery